These ebooks are so exclusive you can't even buy them.
When you download them I'll also send you updates when
new books like this are available.

Again, that link is:

www.saucyromancebooks.com/physical

All Or Nothing

A BWAM billionaire single parent romance

A complete story, brought to you by popular bestselling author Mary Peart.

When billionaire Peter Hamasaki needs his mother's kitchen remodeled, he turns to the people he knows will do the best job: The Faulkner family.

Little did he know he'd be getting more out of the transaction than expected.

Head designer Elise Faulkner is all her could want from a woman: smart, beautiful, and entrepreneurial like himself.

Despite her not wanting to let anyone in too fast, the two soon grow undeniable feelings for each other, and a real future seems far from unrealistic.

But when Elise feels it could be serious and reveals she has a son, how will Peter react?

Will he take her all?

Or will he leave with nothing?

Find out in this heartfelt single parent romance by bestselling author Mary Peart.

Suitable for over 18s only due to sex scenes so hot, you'll want your own Asian billionaire to snuggle up with.

Get Free Romance eBooks!

Hi there. As a special thank you for buying this book, for a limited time I want to send you some great ebooks completely **free of charge** directly to your email! You can get it by going to this page:

www.saucyromancebooks.com/physical

You can see a the cover of these books on the next page:

Contents

Chapter 1

"Hey mom, look what I made!" Four year old Daniel raced towards the door as soon as it opened.

"Honey, what is it?" Elise scooped him up, saving him from crashing headlong into the open door. "And remember, Grandma says no running in the house." she said, ruffling his crazy black curls fondly.

"It's a house, and we made it from fudge sticks." He showed her the poorly constructed house with glue showing everywhere and with a myriad of colors all over it.

"Sweet." she kissed his cheek as he wriggled out of her arms impatiently.

"I can see he is planning on going into the family business," an amused voice sounded in front of them. Leslie Faulkner took off her apron and came towards her daughter and grandson. "Hi honey, you are home early." It was a little past the hour of six and Elise did not usually get home until after eight. She and her crew had been renovating a garage but had run out of materials. The owner told them that she would not be able to get more until tomorrow.

"We ran out of tiles," Elise said with a shrug. Daniel had gone off somewhere in the house to play with his toys. They could hear him making truck noises with his mouth. "How was he today?" she continued, plopping down on the sofa and pulling off her work boots.

"He had a little fever but he has been eating up a storm so I guess he is almost his usual self." Leslie never ceased to be amazed that her petite and beautiful daughter had decided to go into construction like her late father. Despite her size and how delicate she looked, she could swing a hammer and operate a power drill with the best of them and she had a knack for turning something ordinary into something of incredible beauty! "So how was your day?"

"Michael messed up on the measurements of the floor, that's why the tiles ran short," she said grimly, stretching out her legs and wriggling her toes. "The lady was very decent about it but you know I don't work that way mom. I am thinking of letting him go."

"Honey, no!" Leslie exclaimed. "He has been with your father since the inception of the company, it's his life."

"That's why he needs to retire now mom," Elise said impatiently, feeling the guilt flooding through her. "He has been messing up on quite a few jobs and the rest of the crew has been complaining. What else am I supposed to do? I have the reputation of Faulkner's Remodeling to think about."

"How about not letting him do the measuring?" Leslie asked trying to find a solution. Michael Laird had been a part of the company for so long that he was more like family. He had no family of his own to speak of, never having married and children.

"I'll think of something" Elise said wearily, feeling the weight of responsibility on her slim shoulders.

"When are we going to eat?" Daniel raced into the room. "I am starving!"

*****

"How about another story mom, please?" Daniel asked with a pleading look on his freshly scrubbed face. She had given him a bath and placed his favorite stuffed toy, 'Mr. Bear,' beside him and had just read him 'Goodnight Moon'.

She loved this time that she spent with him and realized that because of work she did not get to spend the quality time with him that she wanted to. Her mother was mostly there and although she was happy that her mom was available to pick him up from kindergarten and take him to swimming lessons, she wanted to be the one to do it. He was her son and she was the only parent in his life.

"It's after nine now honey." She told him apologetically. "How about I read you two stories tomorrow?"

"Okay," he said with an impish grin, his dimples peeking out. He looked so much like her and she had always been thankful for that. His father had left as soon as he had discovered that she was pregnant and she had not heard from him since.

"How about a little cuddle for your old lady?" she teased, bending over him.

"You are not old!" he told her staunchly. "My teacher thinks you are very pretty and she can't understand why you are doing a man's job. I want to do the same thing that you do when I grow up, mommy," he turned his handsome little face up to her to be kissed, his tone serious.

"We'll see, baby boy," she kissed him tenderly on both cheeks and nuzzled his hair for a minute, inhaling the baby powder and lotion she had put on him. "Now go to sleep and I will make sure to check for monsters underneath the bed and in the closet."

"Thanks mommy." He brought the comforter up to his chin and closed his eyes as she did the necessary checks and turned out the light.

Her mother was waiting for her in the kitchen with a cup of hot chocolate. It was nearing Halloween and the weather had turned cold. "Is he asleep?" Leslie joined her daughter as she sat around the beautiful marble counter Elise herself had designed and put together.

"He was dozing off while I was looking for monsters," Elise said with a smile. "I just remembered that Halloween is approaching and I have yet to look for a suitable costume for him. I promised that I would carve the pumpkin with him this year. I hate that I am leaving so many things on you mom."

"Honey, you know how I love taking care of my grandson. This weekend if you are not working, we could go to the pumpkin patch to pick out a suitable one for him."

"I miss dad," Elise murmured staring into her half cup of hot chocolate.

"Me too," her mother said patting her hand. "Very much."

*****

Later in her room after she had taken a shower, Elise rubbed the cream into her skin, her expression thoughtful. She had been about six years old when she knew she wanted to be like her father. She had followed him around and watched him turn plain pieces of wood into something beautiful and had seen what he had done to their old shabby bathroom. She remembered calling him a magician and he had laughed and told her that he could not make things disappear.

He had indulged her by buying her a toy tool box and while he was constructing the real thing she was building things from the stuff in her tool box. She had never hankered over dolls, but had always wanted tools and construction paper to draw on and create.

"You are going to turn that child into a mini you," his wife had told him dryly.

"She already is." He had responded with a grin.

He had been such a wonderful father. When he had died just after she had given birth to Daniel, she had been devastated especially since Toby, Daniel's father, had run out on her when she had gotten pregnant. He would have made such a good role model for her son.

She had been so young and stupid! Elise thought with a sigh, replacing the cream on the dresser. He had been an itinerant, who had come in from out of town with his jet black hair and hazel eyes. She had been so smitten that it had taken little effort on his part to seduce her. He had gotten a job with her father while she had been doing apprenticeship work at the company. He had been there for two months before he had taken her virginity on the newly redone floorboards inside a house they were remodeling. He had pledged his undying love to her until two months later when she had told him that she was pregnant. He had held her close to him and let her cry; assuring her that everything was going to be fine. He had left the next morning without a forwarding address. She had dreaded telling her parents but when she had eventually done so, they had been very supportive and helped her through it. She had become wise after that and had refused to even go out with anyone else. Her son came first.

She had taken over the company after her father had died and had worked hard to prove herself, that she was as good as any man or maybe even better. In order to not allow her looks to be distracting, she usually wore overalls and big boots and a cap over her shoulder length black hair. She could not do anything about her smooth coffee and cream complexion nor the fact that her full lips were a little pouty but she stayed away from make-up and girlie clothes. She had maybe two dresses in her small closet and that was enough.

Bundling her hair up in a ponytail, she turned the lights out and went to bed.

*****

The building housing 'Hamasaki Import and Export rose majestically against the skyline uptown with its numerous glass windows reflecting the midday sun. The CEO of the company, Peter Hamasaki, who had taken over for his father three years ago following his death, stood at the huge bay window overlooking the shopping mall. He was awaiting a conference call from Japan and just needed to collect his thoughts a bit. He commanded attention wherever he went, with his tall slim build and his straight dark hair combed ruthlessly back from his broad forehead, and his piercing dark eyes. He was known in the business world as a ruthless businessman who did not suffer fools gladly. He was extremely successful and dressed the part, his suits immaculately and tastefully expensive.

His intercom sounded just then. "Your mother is on the line for you, Mr. Hamasaki," his personal secretary said.

Slightly annoyed but not showing it on his face or in his tone he responded. "Tell her I will call her back shortly, Julia. I am awaiting the call from Japan."

"Yes sir," the woman said respectfully. He never socialized with his staff members, preferring to keep himself aloof. He expected his work to be done at a professional level.

The call came through just then and he went back to his desk.

*****

"Mother, I hope it was nothing too urgent," he said when he returned the call.

"And if it had been then I would have had to wait," Mitsui Hamasaki said dryly. "I have decided to remodel the kitchen. I am just letting you know in case you come home and wonder what's happening."

"What's wrong with the kitchen we currently have?" he asked, not in the least bit interested.

"I want something light and airy Peter, somewhere I can sit and enjoy my tea without thinking that I am in a dungeon." She told him impatiently. Her son was all about business and thought of nothing else and sometimes it got on her nerves at how indifferent he was to everything else.

"Go ahead mother. You certainly do not need my approval." He told her, wanting to get off the phone. He had a shipment of vehicles to be approved before they arrived and he had a board meeting in half an hour; he certainly did not have time to discuss the inappropriate lighting in their kitchen.

"I know I do not need your approval, but your input would be nice." She continued, knowing she was wasting her time by saying it.

"I am sorry mother, but you know the house is your forte." He glanced at the clock on his desk impatiently. "I have to go now."

"Will you be home for dinner?" she asked hopefully, knowing the answer before he responded.

"I am not so sure." He said briefly before hanging up.

*****

Mitsui put down the phone and got to her feet, smiling as she heard the murmur of female voices in the dining room. It was her turn to host their book club meeting and they were at the moment discussing the merits of 'Pride and Prejudice.' She had asked the live in help, Miki to serve them Mocha ice cream and Daifuku, a glutinous rice cake stuffed with sweet filling and a fruit plate with a selection of fruits. The ladies turned to look at her as she re-entered the room. "I swear that I put on an extra five pounds every time I am here for book club, Mitsui," a tall willowy blonde by the name of Angie told her. "I have to abstain from dessert for a whole week after I leave here." She said with a groan. She had eaten more of the delicious pastry than she had wanted to but she had found it hard to resist the tasty fare. "How do you manage to eat all this and still remain so slender?"

"There is a secret to that." Mitsui sat down and crossed her elegantly clad legs, brushing back her still jet black hair. "I don't touch the stuff."

"I am afraid I cannot say the same," Lucy, a chubby red haired woman complained. "I am always touching and tasting and eating."

"You have to practice self control," another woman, Linda said, her bony angular face very serious as she peered at them above her spectacles. "After I leave here, I cleanse myself by drinking a special herbal tea I found in the Chinese store."

The rest of the women stared at her in amusement. "Do you actually read the ingredients that they put in those teas?" Lucy asked her.

"Not really," she said with a shrug. "I just make the tea and drink it and it works every time."

With a shake of her head, Mitsui turned the conversation back to the matter at hand. It was always the same conversation every time and if she did not stop it, they would be sure to continue until someone got offended.

*****

Elise sat back on her haunches and looked at the diagonal pattern of the tiles she had just laid. She had chosen cream with a pink tinge in it and Mrs. Sutherland had approved of it wholeheartedly. Jack, the next member of the crew looked on approvingly. "Looking good girl" he said with a grin. He had also been with the company for a long time but not as long as Michael had been. She had spoken with him this morning and told him he had to scale down and he had given her a look that had her twisting inside with guilt. No matter, it was for the best and she could not afford to let the reputation of the company her father had built, slide. She was thinking of employing someone else to help with the jobs but she was a little hesitant, thinking of Daniel's father. Not that that was going to happen to her again, but you never knew.

She stood up in one fluid movement and handed the trowel to Jack while she went inside the house to talk to Mrs. Sutherland. They were almost finished, only some shelves to be installed at the back of the garage, and Jack would be doing that.

"Good job my dear," the elderly woman told her with a pleased smile. "I have given your card to a friend of mine who is planning on remodeling her kitchen as well, so you can expect a call from her any time now." She handed Elise a glass of lemonade. The men had already had theirs along with some homemade oatmeal cookies. "Now dear, let me get my check book and allow you to get on your way."

*****

"How about this one?"Elise pointed to a pumpkin that was large enough to hold her son inside it. She had taken the weekend off, determined to find a suitable pumpkin for her son and also to go and look for a Halloween costume.

"It is so big!" the boy clapped his hands in delight. "I want it mommy!"
"Of course you do honey," Leslie said with a fond smile, ruffling his curls. He was in his jacket, well zipped up to his chin because the wind had been blowing through the trees adding to the already chilly weather.

They struggled with getting the pumpkin to the car and then headed to the mall. "What kind of costume do you want this year, honey?" She adjusted her mirror to look at him, well secured in the car seat in the back.

"I want to be a ghost!" he said in excitement, his large dark eyes shining, so much like hers.

"Weren't you a ghost last year?" his grandmother asked him, turning around in the front seat to look at him.

"Ghosts are cool because they get to scare people," he told her solemnly.

"I see," his mother looked at him with a smile. "And that's what you want to do? Scare people?"

He nodded vigorously.

"Well, ghost it is then."

They found a scary enough ghost costume for him and afterwards they went to get pizza and hot chocolate at the pizza place.

They were in the middle of eating when Daniel spotted a couple with a child close to his age. He looked at them for a moment before saying, "I wish I had a dad,"

The two women looked at him wordlessly for a moment. He had never expressed that wish before and even though he was so tender in age, she had explained to him that his dad had left because he was not ready to be a father.

Elise felt the anger burn inside her at the bastard who had fled his responsibility and left her to pick up the pieces. She reached out and took his hands, oily from the slices of pizza he had consumed. He had a chocolate mustache on his top lip and she used the napkin to wipe it off. "Honey, remember how I explained to you about not having a dad?" he nodded solemnly. "And I also reminded you that I did not have a dad either and that grandma no longer had a dad? What did you say to me?"

"I will be the man in the house!" he said his eyes sparkling and his mood changing.

"That's right, sweetie," Leslie said exchanging looks with her daughter. "We are happy with the way we are right now and we love one another and that's all that matters."

He nodded."May I have another slice of pizza please?" he asked, already forgetting the subject of his absent father, but Elise was still feeling the anger burning inside her.

"Where do you put all the food?" she teased him, handing him another slice.

"Right in my tummy," he told her with a laugh.

*****

That night as she tucked him into bed he asked her: "Mommy, are you sad that I asked you about a dad?" Elise closed her eyes briefly, she had forgotten how very intuitive he could be and she forced a smile to her lips.

"Of course not darling why would I be sad?" she sat on the bed beside him and held him close to her.

"I don't know," he shrugged slightly, snuggling close to her. "I pray for a daddy sometimes for me and that you won't have to work so hard every day."

Elise felt her throat constricting and she had to take a deep breath in order to continue. "I hope your prayers will be answered." She said huskily. "In the meantime, can you bear with only your mommy for now?"

"Of course mommy, you are the best mommy in the whole wide world!" he told her flinging out his hands to emphasize his point.

"Thanks sweetie. It helps that you are the best son in the whole wide world!" she hugged him before pulling up the comforter and turning out the light.

Her mother had already turned in for the night. Elise went inside her room and dropped herself onto her bed. It was the first time he had ever mentioned needing a father and it pained her that as much as she tried to give him whatever he needed, she could not give him his father.

The bastard had not wanted any part of the beautiful sweet child they had made. She had spent so many nights beating herself up and wondering where she had gone wrong and how she could have fallen for his pretty looks and smooth talk until her mother had sat her down and talked to her.

"You made a mistake honey, and no matter how you try to analyze it, the mistake has already been made. Now you just have to dust yourself off and be there for your son, no matter what, because he is going to need you!"

She had done just that and had moved on from the lousy bastard, but no amount of wishing on her part could erase the fact that he was indeed Daniel's father.

Chapter 2

"Of course Mrs. Hamasaki. I will do up a proposal as soon as I come and look at the place, and thank you very much!" Elise could not keep the excitement out of her voice; she had gotten the job of remodeling the entire kitchen in the Hamasaki's home. It meant quite a bit of income. She knew about the family, had seen them featured in the papers, especially the son Peter who ran the company.

"Please call me Mitsui my dear. Mrs. Hamasaki makes me sound so old." The woman said with a smile in her voice. "So can you come over this afternoon to take a look?"

Elise hesitated briefly, trying to piece together in her head what she had to do. It was already Friday and she had promised her son to go trick or treating later, and she had to finish up a bathroom job as well. "Of course. I will be there this afternoon around two o'clock, if that's okay with you."

"Good," the woman said. "I will be waiting."

"Mom, would you mind taking Daniel to school this morning? I have several things I need to do," she said pulling on her jacket. She had already bathed and gotten her son ready for school. He only needed to eat breakfast. He was already hyped up about Halloween and could not stay still. She told her mother about the potential job.

"Honey, that's great! Of course I will take Daniel to school, and pick him up afterwards. I only have some pastry to deliver to the shop downtown then I am free for the day." Leslie told her.

"Thanks mom." Elise said gratefully.

"Just make sure you do not disappoint little man for later." Her mother warned.

"I won't," Elise reassured her, stooping down as her son flew from the living room and into her arms.
"Mommy, I ate all my pancakes and strawberries!" his mouth had maple syrup and bits of strawberries all around it. There was a syrup stain on his school uniform.
"And you got some of it on your clothes and all over your mouth." She said with an indulgent smile, grabbing a bag of wipes from the side table and cleaning his face with it."Okay buddy, mommy is going to work now so grandma will take you to school and pick you up after, but I will be by later for us to go trick or treating together. How does that sound?" she ruffled his curls as she stood up.

"Sounds good Mommy. Have a good day at work." He told her solemnly.

"Have a super duper day at school honey," she told him with a smile.

*****

"So we got the Hamasaki gig?" Jack asked, his dark brown eyes squinting as he examined the tiles he had just laid.

"Hopefully." Elise looked at the tiles briefly. The bathroom had been gutted completely and everything, including the dingy tub, face basin and toilet fixtures, had been removed and replaced with powder blue fixtures with beautiful chrome fittings, and matching blue and white tiles on the floor and on the walls. She especially loved the sea nymphs patterned on the top of the tiles on the wall. "I have to go look at the place and get a feel of what we need to do."

"Want me to tag along?" he asked her, wiping his hands on his already messy denims. Michael was cleaning the grout off the tiles and not saying anything. Ever since she had scaled down his duties he had been taciturn and surly.

"No, I can take care of it. You guys have the portico to finish remember?" she reminded him.

"Oh yes, I had forgotten about that." He said slapping his gloves on his thigh.

"I will let you know how it goes." She told him briefly.

*****

"Come on in dear," the woman told her as she met her in the driveway. It was a cold and blustery day and wind had whipped at her loose ponytail and now her hair was all over the place. The place was massive with a circular driveway and cobbled stones on the walls out front. It was beautiful and the grounds were well kept. "Now I am going to ask you the obvious question: why is a beautiful girl like you doing such rough work?" Mitsui glided in front of her, her curtain of fine black hair raining down her back as she led them through a large parlor, an elegant living room with shimmering chandeliers and a sweeping staircase at one end, and into the large kitchen, big enough to be used in a restaurant.

"I like what I do," she told her politely, her eyes quickly assessing what needed to stay and what should go.

Page 29

"Ah, I have been put in my place." Mitsui said in amusement. "My son is always telling me that I am too nosy."

"No, I am sorry. I tend to get distracted when I am on a job." Elise told her apologetically giving the woman a tentative smile.

"So what do you think?" she asked sweeping her hands to encompass the room. The lighting was poor, but it was due to the lack of windows, and the wallpaper was too dark and dreary. The marble countertop was exquisite and Elise was sure it had cost a pretty penny. The chrome fittings were some of the best. The floor was made of highly polished wood and shone beautifully.

"I think we should put a large bay window right there." She pointed to the area above the sink. "And another one over there." She indicated the opposite side of the room. "The wallpaper needs to go. We could put tiles instead, and if you want I could add a little breakfast nook right in the middle."

"My thoughts exactly." Mitsui nodded in approval. "We have two more kitchens in this veritable mansion, one on the east wing and the other on the south, which belongs to my son. He never uses the place because he spends more time in the office than here and he never cooks for himself, but I would like you to do those as well."

Elise could feel the excitement rising inside her. Three kitchens in this massive house? And who's to tell if there won't be other jobs as long as they do excellent work? It would mean money going into her son's college fund!

"How soon do you want me to start?" she asked, impatient to get started.

"How about tomorrow?" Mitsui asked with a smile. "I will just instruct the girls to move their things out so that you can have space to do your work."
"That sounds great!" Elise said with a quick smile.

"And my dear, you don't need to spare any expense.. I want the very best." Mitsui told her.

*****

"Stand still sweetie, I need to put the hood over your head. No self-respecting ghost would go without it." Elise secured the material over his head making sure it was not too tight and pulled down the sleeves of his white sweater down to his wrists. It was cold out and she was making sure he was warm enough.

"Mommy, you are funny," his teeth flashed white inside the opening through the material. "Do I look scary?"

"I am scared right now," she said with a little shiver.

"Boo!" he said.

"Stop you are going to give me a heart attack!" his mother held a hand to her chest.

"And me as well," Leslie said coming into the living room with a basket full of candies and various treats. "Here you go darling, make sure you don't come back with any of these."

"Thanks Grandma. Mommy, come on! We are going to be late." He said tugging her hand impatiently.

"Okay buddy, I am coming."

"I will hold down the fort here until you two are back." Leslie told them as they went through the doorway.

*****

Darkness had already descended. Even though it was only a few minutes after six o'clock, she could see other mothers and some fathers with their small children in tow. The costumes were many and varied and she even saw that there were several other 'ghosts' milling around.

Her energetic son dragged her around the neighborhood handing out treats and trying to trick people into believing he was a ghost. She looked at her watch and realized that it was almost nine o'clock and the overflowing basket was empty.

"Mommy, we are out of treats," he told her worriedly, holding up the empty basket.

"And we are also out of time." She told him gently, waving to a parent she recognized. "It's past your bedtime honey."

"Okay mommy," he look wilted and Elise picked him up into her arms, thinking to herself how heavy he had become.

Before they had reached the house he was fast asleep in her arms. She shifted his weight to her right so she could open the door and go in.

"All tuckered out?" her mother came over and took him from her. "Go on honey, I will tuck him in tonight."

"Thanks Mom, he is quite a handful."

*****

The job commenced the very next day with the measuring and the knocking down of the walls to accommodate the windows. They had arrived at a quarter to seven and had been offered breakfast in the form of a buffet, with a variety of dishes including pancakes with maple syrup and strawberries, eggs and lightly browned toast, and flaky, delectable croissants.

"I was not sure what you ate so I told Miki and Linda that they could not go wrong with a continental breakfast," Mitsui told them with a charming smile, shaking Michael's and Jack's hands as they were introduced. "Please make yourselves at home. The two ladies will get you anything you need. I have to run out to get some things done. My son has already left for the office."

"Classy lady," Jack commented, his eyes eagerly going to the table laden with food, sniffing the scent of coffee. "Do we eat first?" he asked hopefully.

"Go ahead," Elise suggested even though she was impatient on getting started.

She poured herself a cup of coffee while the two men ate, and wandered into the kitchen, seeing in her mind's eyes what the finished product will look like.

It was half an hour later before they got started. Elise did the measuring while Michael and Jack got ready to remove the walls. She had already ordered the necessary supplies from the hardware and were going to be delivered as soon as the place was opened. Usually she got the run around whenever she placed an order and had to wait a bit for the order to be filled, but apparently the Hamasaki name carried a lot of weight.

It was mid afternoon before the real work started. They had settled down to have lunch, which had been placed on the table where the breakfast things had been removed.

"What a feast!" Jack said clapping his hands as he viewed the table filled with lots of goodies. There were several different kinds of large chunky sandwiches, a fruit bowl, jugs of lemonade and fruit juice, a whole chocolate cake with vanilla icing, and a pot of coffee. They had seen the two helpers briefly but never saw them putting the food on the table.

"It's almost like a food fairy takes the food here and then returns for the empty plates." Michael said slowly, picking up a chicken sandwich and putting it on a plate.

"Was that a joke from you man?" Jack demanded, clapping Michael on the back.

The man gave a slow smile and ambled over to the corner of the room to eat his lunch.

*****

By the time Mitsui returned,which was after three, Elise and the two men were laying the tiles. She had chosen pale lemon tiles with fruits and vegetables inlaid.

"Looking good already and it's not yet done," Mitsui exclaimed. Elise admired the elegant way she carried herself and the subtle expensive pants suit she had on. "How long is it going to take?" she asked staying just inside the doorway away from the dust.

"We should be finished by Wednesday. We are going to start on the other kitchens as soon as we are done in here." Elise told her.

"Good," she nodded. "Let me know when you are ready to leave and I will come down. Linda and Miki will take the message up. And please do not think you should be here working until six o'clock or after. I am sure you have lives to go home to."

"As I said, classy woman," Jack commented, staring after her.

*****

They wrapped up at a quarter to six and Elise told the helper, Miki, who was a young oriental girl with long black hair to her waist, that they were ready to leave. She nodded and bowed and then hurried off to get her mistress.

Mitsui had changed into red silk lounge pants and a blue shirt and she came down to see them off. "I hope you had something to eat before you leave," she told them accompanying them to the door. "I was so caught up in some paperwork I was doing that I completely lost track of time."

"Yes, thank you very much." Elise told her with a smile. She was feeling grimy and badly needed a shower and to wash out the dust and the grout out of her hair.

"Okay I will see you tomorrow." She said waving them off.

*****

Elise told her mother about the house. They were having their meal around the dining table, and she watched as her son picked at his brussel sprouts. He had eaten the fried chicken and corn but was trying not to eat the other vegetable.

"Sweetie don't you want to get big and strong?" Elise asked him gently as he stared at the vegetable fiercely.

"Yes, but why do I have to eat this? It's so icky!" he said mutinously.

"How about this?" his grandmother suggested. "Eat at least three bites and then you will get a chocolate chip cookie and a little bit of ice cream."
His eyes brightened as he looked at the two women. "Can I mommy, please?"

"May I," she corrected automatically. Usually she did not allow sweets before bedtime but she decided it would not hurt. "Okay but you have to try and eat all of the vegetable."

"Okay," he scooped the vegetable put inside mouth and before long he had finished everything on his plate.

"Good job, honey." His grandma told him with a smile, getting up to go and get dessert. The grownups had coffee with cream and cookies and he had his ice-cream and two cookies.

She had made sure he brushed his teeth and had tucked him into bed before she came back out to join her mother on the sofa in the living room, pouring herself another cup of coffee.

"The house is a dream mom. It looks mellowed and old and had been redesigned over the years but it is a magnificent building and the grounds are so big, at least what I caught a glimpse of."

"I am glad you were able to get the job, honey," Leslie said with a smile. "How is the lady of the house?"

"Very nice for a rich lady, according to Jack," she said with a laugh. "I haven't met the son yet because his mother says he spends most time at the office."

Later that night as she prepared for bed, she reflected back on the glimpses of luxury she had seen in the house. The rich oak paneling in the parlor, the parquet floors and the various works of art hanging on the walls. She had recognized Renoir and Monet and several others that she had not recognized but seemed to be highly expensive. She had never wondered what it was like to live in houses of such grandeur but she loved the feel of a beautiful piece of wood in her hands, and she had learned to appreciate fine things from her father. What does one do in a house that size for the whole day? She wondered, shaking her head as she slipped on her simple cotton nightgown with the intention of going to bed.

*****

Peter hung up his jacket on the pole just inside the parlor and flexed his shoulder muscles wearily. He had just left the office and it was now almost nine thirty and all he wanted to do was take a shower and go straight to bed.

"You could have called," Mitsui said accusingly, turning on the light in the living room as he came in.

"Hello mother," he said, in the way of greeting, not in the least bit in the mood for reprimands. He should have taken the staircase around his side of the residence but she always wants to know that he was home safely so he humored her. "I did not get a chance to do so. Why are you still up?"

Mitsui shook her head slightly. Her son was going to be the death of her. "I was waiting up for you Peter, and despite being the adult big shot you are, the fact remains that you are still my son and I get concerned."

"No need to be concerned mother, you know where I am." Peter made as if to leave.

"The work on the kitchen started today, don't you want to see what's being done?" Mitsui asked him.

He closed his eyes and stifled his impatience. "Of course." He followed her into the kitchen. All he saw was the dust in the corner and the gutted out walls.

"They have not done much have they?" he observed, his piercing dark eyes taking in the tools left in the corner of the room. "Have they come highly qualified? Did you check them out to see if they are legitimate?"

Mitsui let out a peal of laughter that had him turning to face her. "My son the businessman. Her name is Elise Faulkner, and she is the owner of Faulkner's Remodeling, so you can go ahead and see if she is legit."

"A woman is doing this?" he turned back to look at the place with a frown.

"Yes darling, a woman and two men, but she is in charge." Mitsui said in amusement.

"Mother, I am sure there are highly qualified people you could have hired. Does this woman know what she is doing?"

"Why, because she is a woman?" Mitsui asked him, her eyes so much like his own looking at him. "Careful darling, your prejudice is showing."

"I am not-" he stopped before he uttered the word. What the hell. It was her project and he had no intention of getting involved. "It's your thing mother, so I won't interfere."

"Thanks darling for your support as usual," she told him dryly as he left the room.

He did not answer but continued on his way until he entered his suite of rooms. He closed the door behind him with a sigh and went into the master bedroom. The suite had three bedrooms, a living room, a den, two bathrooms and a kitchen and dining room, not that he ever used the kitchen. When he was entertaining guests from overseas, he used the main dining room. He had a back and front balcony that overlooked the gardens and sometimes he would go sit out on one of them and have himself a glass of wine and just meditate. He was not into a serious relationship, not having the time and patience to put in the effort of building one, but he enjoyed the company of women when he felt the need. He never took them to where he lived, preferring to take them to a lovely little cottage on the other side of town. He did not want them to get the wrong idea of it being something permanent. He knew his mother despaired of him settling down and giving her grandchildren, but he had no intention of granting her wish just because she wanted to be a grandmother. There was still time for him to settle down; after all he was only twenty seven.

He poured the wine that had been left in the wine cooler into a glass and went out on the balcony at the back. It was a bit cold but he had put on his thick robe. Taking a seat, he settled down to enjoy the night.

Chapter 3

Elise was sitting Indian style on the floor, looking at the drawing she had done, a little furrow on her usually smooth brow. It was Tuesday and the job was slated to be finished by tomorrow. Both Michael and Jack had gone on to add the finishing touch to a small bathroom they had been assigned to do. The breakfast nook was almost finished and the marble counter top shone brightly in the light coming from outside. It was almost six o'clock but she wanted to finish to a certain point before tomorrow. The two helpers had retired for the evening but had told her to just ring the bell when she was ready to leave. Mitsui had gone out to a charity function and had told her that she would see her tomorrow.

That was how Peter saw her, sitting there on his kitchen floor with her head bent over something. She was so intent on whatever it was she was reading or studying that she did not hear him come in.

"Ms. Faulkner I take it?"

Her head snapped up and Peter was stunned by the natural raw beauty of her face. Her large dark brown eyes looked at him directly, and even though she was not wearing make-up, she was the most beautiful woman he had ever laid eyes on. Her hair was messy, he thought objectively, and she was wearing an army green shirt that was too big for her small frame.

"Mr. Hamasaki I take it?" her soft fluid voice was tinged with amusement and he realized that she did not jump to her feet even though she realized who he was.

"Yes," he told her briefly, coming into the room. She still had not gotten up and he wondered if she was always this rude. "Isn't it a bit late to be doing this?" he gestured with his hands at the work that was done. He realized with grudging admiration that the kitchen looked far better than it had before.

"You mean remodeling?" she asked him. He was far better looking than his pictures in the papers and he looked taller but he needed to lose the frown on his brow. "Your mother said I could go ahead. I want to finish with the breakfast nook before I leave." She finally stood up in one graceful movement and went over to run her hand over the marble counter top. "So what do you think?" she asked him, carelessly reaching up to secure her curls back into a ponytail. Her lips were devoid of artifice and they looked very inviting.

He shook his head as if to clear it and looked around the room. "It's pretty impressive." He told her.

"You sound as if you did not expect it to be," her voice was amused as she looked at him.

"I didn't," he admitted truthfully, his piercing dark eyes holding hers.

"Why? Because I am female?" she asked her brows arched.

"Because I am not familiar with your work, Ms. Faulkner," he said coolly.

"Ah," she bit back a smile. "I am not some big name with multimillion contracts and a boat load of men to command, is that it?"

He gave her a fulminating stare. She was impudent, and he was not used to women being that way. He usually called all the shots and he was always in command. "I am impressed Ms. Faulkner, take it in the spirit it was said." He told her coolly.

"Now I can sleep in my bed tonight knowing you are impressed." She started to unbutton the shirt, and for one startled moment Peter thought she was undressing in front of him. "Relax Mr. Hamasaki," she said, seeing his expression. "I am just changing out of my work shirt and putting on my street clothes." She shrugged out of the shirt and stood before him, wearing a thin camisole and denims that hugged her curvaceous figure like a glove. He got a glimpse of her generous breast before she pulled a T-shirt over her head. "Tell your mother I will see her tomorrow." She told him briefly before taking up her tool belt and heading out.

He stood there like an idiot and watched her as she walked out, her strides long and confident for such a small person. He had never met anyone like her. He found himself going to the window and peering out like a schoolboy with his first crush and watched as she climbed into the old Chevrolet van and drove away.

His expression was thoughtful as he went back inside the kitchen. He was impressed by her work, but more so by her.

*****

"Mommy can you help me make a house?" Daniel asked, jumping on the living room sofa where she was sitting and reading a proposal. She wanted to do the other two kitchens different from the main kitchen and she was brainstorming.

"I thought you already knew how to," she put away the document and gave him her full attention. He was already bathed and in his adorable pajamas with colorful pictures of Winnie the Pooh all over it.

"I can, but you make it gooder," he told her hopping into her lap.

"Better," she corrected him. "Why do you want to make a house?"

"Because I want to be like you and grandpa, so I want to learn." He told her solemnly.

"Okay buddy, how about this weekend we make it an assignment?" she sat him on her lap and looked at him fondly.

"What's an 'signment?" he asked with a frown.

"Assignment," she told him with a smile. "It's kind of like homework."

"Oh, like what we get to do from Ms. Blake?" he asked her.

"Exactly." She said hugging him.

"Okay, but what about the things we need to make the house?" he asked a little worried.

"I think I might have some stuff in the garage." She assured him.

"Good!" he said clapping his hands in delight.

*****

Peter left the office early telling himself that it was not because he wanted to see her again, it was due to the fact that he wanted go over some contracts and he needed the quietness of his own suite of rooms. It was a little past five; he was not known to be home so early.

"Darling why are you home so early? Are you ill?" was the first thing his mother greeted him with. It did not help that Elise was standing inside the kitchen as well.

"No mother, I don't have to be ill to be home early," he felt like he was under a damn microscope.

"Have you met Elise?" she asked him.

"Yes, we met last evening," he said, surprised that she had not told his mother that she had seen him.

"Oh, so what do you think?" she did not wait for him to say anything. "I was telling Elise that if she does not watch out, I will be hiring her full time."

"I have no problem with that." Elise was looking at him curiously and he realized that he had come straight into the kitchen with his cashmere coat on.

"It looks well done mother," he told her and was rewarded with a big smile.

"They are finished up in here now and will be tackling your kitchen and the kitchen in the east wing next."

He opened his mouth to tell her that he never used his kitchen so what was the sense, but for some reason he kept it closed. "Do you want to have a look at it?" he heard himself asking.

Both women turned to look at him in surprise and he could have kicked himself.

"Of course," Elise nodded.

"Okay, you two go ahead and I will head on upstairs to get ready. I have that dinner with the ladies of the book club to go to. We are celebrating our tenth book." Mitsui said with a smile.

"My mother is the member of a book club," he told her with a lack of something to say.

"So I gathered," her voice was tinged with amusement.

He led the rest of the way in complete silence, afraid that he was going to put his foot in his mouth again.

Elise found herself admiring the architecture and finish of the place. His suite was entirely masculine and as she passed through the living room she found herself drawn to the intricately designed fireplace. "This is beautiful," she said running a hand over the beautifully carved wood of the mantel.

"It came with the house," he told her, watching as she ran a hand slowly over the piece of wood, her face animated.

"The whole place was well built," she said looking around at the beautiful wood paneling as she continued on into the kitchen. It was plain and utilitarian and the only saving grace was the beautiful counter top that took curved around the room. The place looked as if it had never been used for years. "Do you actually use this kitchen?" she turned and gave him a direct look. He was close behind her and he could smell her scent of wood and something strawberry-like.

"I don't cook," he told her honestly stepping back from her. The closeness was starting to make him feel uncomfortable.

"So why do you want to remodel?" she had to tilt her head to look up at him and the fact that she was wearing sneakers made it worse.

"You never know, I might decide to start cooking one day," he said with a shrug.

"I see," she turned back to look at the room. "Any ideas?'

"No, I am leaving it entirely up to you."

"Good idea" she said in amusement. "So I am given carte blanche with this project?"

"Absolutely." He told her. She was not wearing the work shirt but had on a black T-shirt that looked startling against her coffee and cream complexion, her hair in its usual ponytail.

She fished a notepad and pencil from her back pocket and started taking notes, forgetting that he was in the room. He used the opportunity to look at her closely. She had long lashes and her lips moved as she muttered something to herself. She had long fingers that moved swiftly over the paper.

She looked up suddenly and caught his eyes, her expression quizzical as she noticed him staring at her.
"Do you always talk to yourself when you are working?" he asked quickly, trying to make it seem like he was fascinated by her habit instead of by her.

"It's a dreadful fault of mine," she laughed and his breath caught. Her eyes brightened and the laughter lit up her beautiful face. "I have to be going now, my son awaits."

"You have a son?" he asked frowning a little and taken off guard. Did it mean she was married?

"Yes I have a four year old who is the love of my life." She admitted.

"So, does your husband approve of the job you do?" he asked her casually in an attempt to find out.

"I am not married Mr. Hamasaki. I am a single mom." She told him with a lift of her shoulders.

He felt his spirits soar! What the hell was he doing? She was not his type and she had a kid, definitely not for him.

"Call me Peter, please," he heard himself telling her.

"The name is Elise," she said briefly, turning to leave.

"So we will be seeing you tomorrow?" he asked following behind her; loathe to see her leave.

"You are usually at the office when I am here. Your mother says you work non-stop." She told him in amusement.

Damn mother and her loose mouth! He thought in frustration.

"I want to see what you are doing with the place." He said.

"Okay see you tomorrow," she told him with a little wave heading out the door.

He found himself peering at her through the drapes and cursing himself for being so foolish!

*****

Elise had written up some ideas on how she wanted to do his kitchen. He was male, and she had caught glimpses of the bedrooms and the totally male bathroom with their glossy black and white tiles, and decided to do it up in tan and burgundy. Male domain or not, a kitchen was supposed to be cheerful. She got there at seven thirty and Mitsui told her that Peter was still around. Michael and Jack were coming by later.

"I thought he would have left by now," Elise said with a slight frown.

"I thought so too, my dear," she looked at the girl considering for a little bit. Ever since the meeting with Elise, her son had been behaving strangely. He had come home early yesterday and usually she would wake up and find him already gone to work, but he was still at home. "Go on up, I guess he is waiting for you to show him what you have so far."

"Okay, I will see you in a little bit." She said striding quickly in the direction of Peter's suite.

She was beautiful, Mitsui thought, staring after her. She was unusual, and she was not in the least bit impressed by their wealth. A little smile played around her mouth as she went back to her suite to get ready to go out; maybe Peter had finally met his match.

*****

He had on his lavender dress shirt and purple and white tie and was standing in the kitchen as if he was waiting on her. "Hi I did not expect to see you." He had watched her walk towards him. What was it about her? She had no make-up on and was wearing a powder blue T-shirt; she had obviously left her jacket downstairs, and was wearing the usual faded denims.

"I wanted to see what you came up with," he told her swiftly.

"Afraid I am going to come up with a pink and white color scheme?" she asked him in amusement, coming to stand next to him and opening her notebook.

"Something like that," he told her lightly, her nearness having a profound effect on him.

"Don't worry, I hate pink myself and don't impose it on anyone unless they specifically ask for it." She showed him samples of the color. "I notice the color scheme in here but I figured you would want something more cheerful for the kitchen."

He was not listening to her and he realized that he wanted to kiss her. What the hell was wrong with him?

"That's fine," he told her briefly, moving back a little. She was too near. "I just remembered I have an early meeting, so I have to go."

"Will I be seeing you later?" she asked him, not having a clue to what was happening with him.

"What?" he looked at her, startled.

"I figured you would like to see what I have done so far, because I am thinking of adding tiles all around the area where the sink is." She told him.

"I am not sure what my day will be like." He told her briefly. He needed to get out of there, and fast.

"Okay, see you then." She waved her hand a little and turned to look at the notes she had in her hand. He stood there looking at her for a brief moment without her being aware that he was doing so. Her head was bent and he saw the curls at the back of her neck and the way the denim cupped her butt lovingly. He went into his room and grabbed his jacket and headed out.

"So, did everything meet your approval?" his mother's voice brought him up short just as he reached the foyer.

"Mother, I thought you had already left." He said, looking and feeling a little guilty.

"I am on my way out but I am curious as to why you are still here. You have no interest in the remodeling and even though she is doing your kitchen, you have never used it so I asked myself: why is he so interested in what color tiles are placed on the walls?" she asked him, one eyebrow arched curiously.

"I might be planning to use it in the future," he shrugged into his jacket and put his hand on the doorknob, regretting that he had not taken the other route.

"I see." Mitsui gave him a knowing look. "So, will we be seeing you early this evening?"

"I don't know what my day will be like mother," he told her impatiently before pulling open the door and letting himself out.

"Of course you don't," she murmured with a wide smile. With a spring in her step she went into the kitchen to tell Miki what to prepare for dinner.

*****

Michael and Jack came by at nine and they started the tough job of removing the tiles that were already there. The floor was also made of parquet and the countertop was a beautiful marble. There was an island in the center and she decided that it would match with the color scheme she was doing. She sat on the floor and was deciding how to lay the tiles. Mitsui had popped inside and told her that she would be out for a little bit and that Miki and Linda would bring lunch up for them but they should raid her son's fridge if they were hungry. "He usually keeps just water and juice in there but I had asked the ladies to stock it up." With a wave she had left.

"It's such a pleasure to work for a lady like that one," Jack said chipping away at the tiles. "Such a classy and caring lady."

"I think Jack is quite taken with her," Michael said to Elise with a grin. He had come around and was talking more, and for that Elise was happy. He had been like a surrogate father to her and he had no one else but them.

"I think he is," Elise agreed with a smirk.

"Cut it out you two!"Jack ordered darkly, chipping away vigorously. "I am just making an observation."

By mid afternoon the broken tiles were on a heap on the floor and they had started to put the new ones up. They had taken a break when lunch was brought up for them and ate and relaxed a little before starting to work again. The tiles were laid with painstaking care and Elise made sure that they were done to perfection; she always told her crew that it was better to stay extra time on the job and get it done properly than to hasten it and it was not done properly.

*****

Peter sat in the meeting and twirled the pen he had in his hand. The shipment of vehicles had come in and had been cleared and was now waiting for inspections from his team of expert mechanics. He already had orders for the high end vehicles and they needed to be sorted out, but he could not concentrate on what was being said. The sales team was giving their report and the finance department had just reported profit in the high nineties. He had nodded and made the necessary noises, but his mind was far away. He was thinking about her and how she had made him feel while he was standing next to her. He had wanted so much to kiss her and he had avoided doing so just in time. He wondered what she would have done if he had carried out his wish; probably knee him in the groins. She looked like the type of woman who would do that.

*****

Elise got the call at two, just as they were laying a fresh batch of tiles. "What's up mom?" she asked swiftly.

"I picked up Daniel from school honey, he's running a temperature." Leslie told her.

"I'll be right there," she said briefly.

"Honey, he is okay now. I gave him a sponge bath and he is drinking some soup and watching his favorite cartoon." Leslie protested.

"I am still coming home, mom." She said, her tone firm. "We are done here for the day, guys. We will start back tomorrow. You can go and look at the next job downtown if you want or you could take the rest of the day and go and drink a couple of beers."

"Sounds fine to me," Jack said with a grin. "How about it, Mike?" he slapped the middle-aged man on the shoulder playfully.

"I think that's a good idea." He said slowly. "Say hello to Danny boy for me." He said with a smile at her.

"I will," she told him warmly and then hurried out. Her son needed her!

Chapter 4

He called her that night. She had just put Daniel to bed and was sipping some herbal tea in the kitchen when she got the call. "Hello?" she frowned at the unfamiliar number, wondering who could be calling her this late. A quick glance at the clock in the kitchen told her it was after nine.

"It's Peter Hamasaki," the deep authoritative voice said. "I understand you had to leave early because your son was not feeling well. How is he?"

Elise did not reply, surprised that he cared enough to call. "It was just a touch of fever but he is fine now. Thanks for calling."

"Well yes, you told me you are a single mom and I was thinking that must be hard on you." He responded.

"I do okay," she said with a small smile. "My mom helps out a lot."

"I see" he hesitated a while as if he was wondering what to say. "I like what I see so far, in the kitchen I mean," he hastened to add.

"I am glad you do." She told him in amusement. "I will be there early in the morning to see how far I can get."

"You will?" he asked wonderingly. "Will your son be well enough for you to leave?"

"He is already driving us crazy," she said in an indulgent voice. "Children are very resilient, they bounce back quickly."

"I guess they are. So I will see you tomorrow then." He said briefly.

"Sure," Elise said before hanging up.

She resumed sipping her tea contemplatively. That was very nice of him to call, she thought in appreciation. She had come home to see her son watching television and eating a hot dog. Her mother had given her a telling glance as if to say I told you so, but even though her mother was such a big help and did not mind doing anything for her grandson, Elise was still very much aware that she was Daniel's mother and the only parent in his life and she took her responsibility seriously. The beauty about her working for herself was that if anything happened she could always leave and come and take care of him, and she was grateful for that. She knew of several single mothers who were having a hard time finding the time to spend with their children and she was glad she had her mother around. The thought of putting Daniel in a daycare center had never appealed to her the slightest bit.

"Hey mommy, what are you doing home so early?" he had looked up at her in surprise, barely taking his eyes off his cartoon.

"I heard a little boy was not feeling well." Elise told him, hunkering down in front of him and looking at him keenly.

"I am fine now. Grandma gave me a bath and medicine and I feel so much better." He had stopped looking at her and was looking at the antics of the cat and the mouse on the television.

"Good to know, honey." She said wryly, kissing him on his cute little nose.

She finished the tea and went to bed, yawning and stretching her aching muscles, thinking about the job at hand tomorrow.

*****

Peter swirled the amber liquid inside the glass and looked at it broodingly. He had no idea what was wrong with him. He had been in total control of his life before now, before he had seen her sitting on his kitchen floor, and now he was doing a lot of things that he had never done before: rushing home from work just to see her and feeling the weight of disappointment when he had reached home only to be told that she was not there, and to make things worse, calling to find out how her son was just so he could hear her voice.

His mother had looked at him strangely when he had asked for her number. He had told her he had some questions about what she had done but he doubted she believed him. He pulled the thick robe around him as he felt the cold penetrate the material. There was a stiff breeze blowing and he knew that very soon he would have to go inside, but he did his thinking better outside on the balcony. He was interested in her and he did not know what he was going to do about it.

*****

Elise propped up against one side of the cupboards with their many drawers, and looked at the work already done. The burgundy and tan ceramic tiles looked very good against the two toned wood. It was a little after six and Michael and Jack had already left but she had stayed back to do some fine tuning. Mitsui had gone to another charity event and had told her that she could stay as long as she wanted.

She turned her head as she heard footsteps in the hallway, smiling languidly as she saw that it was Peter. "Hi there," she called to him.

He stopped right there in the doorway his eyes on her. She was sitting with her legs curled underneath her and she had obviously just taken off her work shirt and was in a thin see through blue camisole where he could see the outline of her generous breasts. "Do you always make a habit of sitting on floors?" he forced his voice to remain light as he came inside the room. He had stayed at the office, thinking that she would have gone by now. He did not know how to act around her and he was afraid of doing something foolish; like closing his mouth over hers.

"Most of the times, yes," she told him with a smile. "I want to look at it from this angle," she added. "Why don't you join me?"

"Pardon me?" he looked at her startled. He still had on his jacket suit; an expensive silver gray tweed and burgundy cotton shirt and gray tie.

"Oh, you don't want to get your expensive suit dirty," she said with a daring grin. "I get it."

He took off his jacket and draped it over one of the stools and loosened his tie and crouched down on the floor beside her.

"Bravo!" she said with a laugh, clapping her hands. "You are not going to have a fit when I leave here are you?" she turned to him, arching a brow.

"I just might," he told her with a smile, loving the way her full lips devoid of make-up, curved over her white teeth. Her hair had become undone and several curls were on her cheeks and the base of her shoulder. "How is your son?" he forced his gaze away from her lips.

"More than okay," she said with a shake of her head, surprised and pleased that he had asked. "He jumped on the bed early this morning and woke me up, telling me he wanted pancakes with strawberries."

"Proving that he is all better," Peter said softly. He hesitated a fraction and asked her the question that had been burning a hole in his gut. "What happened to his father, if you don't mind my asking?"

She shrugged and looked away for a bit. "I was young and foolish and fell for a guy with a pretty look and smooth talk. He left as soon as he found out I was pregnant."

"I am sorry," he sounded sincere and Elise turned her head to look at him, going still as something in his eyes captured her interest.

"That's okay, I have moved on and my son is a delight to me, so no regrets there." She said with a shrug.

"I am sorry you had to go through that," he said softly. There it was again, the intensity and something else she could not identify. The atmosphere was charged with electricity and Elise had the urge to leave but she could not budge.

"I tried to stay away," he continued, one hand reaching out to cup her cheek. "I deliberately stayed at work because I was thinking that maybe you would have already left." Elise could not breathe and she felt her flesh getting hot. He used a thumb to caress her lips.

"Peter-"she began but before she could continue he bent his head and took her lips with his. Elise opened her mouth automatically and with a groan he deepened the kiss! She felt the feelings explode inside her as his tongue met hers. She had been with one other man and it had been only a few times but now she felt as if she was drowning as his mouth moved over hers hungrily. He braced her back gently onto the floor and lay on top of her, his mouth delving inside hers, his body pressing against hers. She gave in to the kiss, her emotions spiraling out of control. He eased away from her, his mouth still on hers and reached underneath her T-shirt to touch her breast. Elise moaned inside his mouth and when he pushed up her lace bra and touched her already hard nipple she felt as if she was going to explode! Somewhere in the fog of emotions swirling around her she found the strength to push him away forcibly, hurriedly getting up, her breathing shallow. He stood up and would have reached for her but she shook her head frantically. "No!" she bit out, her body trembling. "Don't you dare touch me."

"Elise," he opened his mouth to apologize and closed it, knowing it would have been false. "We both wanted it." He said instead.

"Oh is that so?" she asked her voice dangerously soft, her large dark brown eyes flashing. "Mr. Big Shot Billionaire, you think that you can have any woman you want. Or is it the fact that I have a son without a man around, you think I am an easy lay?"

He stepped back as if she had struck him and shoved his hands through his normally tidy dark hair. "That's an unfair thing to say," he told her harshly, giving her a frustrated look.

"Is it?" she drawled in amusement, "I am a novelty to you, a working girl doing a 'man's' job so you wanted to know what it felt like to bed somebody like me, is that it?"

"Stop!" he said harshly causing her to jump a little bit. "It is not like that and you know it."

"I don't know anything," she folded her arms across her chest. "I am not looking for a relationship or to jump into bed with the first available man, so you are looking at the wrong girl. I just want to do my job and get back to my son."

They stood there staring at each other and Elise was the first one to move. She picked up her work shirt and pulled it on and without a word she hurried from the room leaving him staring after her!

Elise climbed inside her truck and sat there without turning the key into the ignition. The imprint of his body was still on hers and she could still feel his mouth on hers. How dare he! She thought angrily. How dare he think she was easy bait and because he was rich she would be willing to drop her panties for him! She had made the mistake of letting a man get too near to her and it will never happen again! She was way too smart now!

She drove home in a daze, hardly concentrating on the road, not noticing the fine rain drizzling on the windshield. It was the first week of November and weather had gotten decidedly chilly. She reached home and parked the vehicle inside the garage and sat there for a while thinking, her thoughts confused. What if he decided not to use her to finish the job? What would she tell the men?

With a sigh she hopped from the vehicle and went inside, forcing a smile as her son launched himself into her arms. "Mommy, I made a toy train at school today and teacher said that mine was the bestest!" he told her in excitement. He was growing so big and it broke her heart to think that his father wanted nothing to do with him.

"Best," she corrected him automatically. "Hi mom," she greeted her mother who had come out of the kitchen to find out what the commotion was all about. "So where is this train?"

"At school," he wriggled out of her arms and went to sit on the sofa where he had been watching his cartoon. "I am hungry. When are we going to eat?" he complained.

"Right after you go and washed those dirty hands of yours," Leslie told him.

He hopped off the sofa and raced away leaving the two women staring after him. "So how was your day?" her mother asked as she busied herself setting the table.

"It was all right," Elise said with a shrug, wondering what her mother would say if she told her that she had been on the kitchen floor with Peter Hamasaki on top of her. "The work is going good. Is that meat loaf I smell?" she asked sniffing the air and wanting to change the subject.

"It sure is." Leslie said with a smile. "Go wash up and let's eat."

*****

Peter stood under the tepid water in the shower, his head bent, letting the water beat down on him. He had watched her leave and had wanted to stop her but how could he? She had made herself clear. He had touched her because he could not help it and now he was paying the price. He had felt the pain of his erection and he closed his eyes as he remembered how she had felt beneath him, how her lips had felt against his and her breasts! He groaned as he recalled touching the hard nipple. He had no doubt that she did not want to see him again. Well that was too damn bad, because if he judged her correctly, she would leave without finishing the job.

*****

Elsie worked in silence while the two men ribbed each other about some card game they had lost. Mitsui had come in briefly and admired the work so far and had gone back to her book club meeting. He had not been there when she came and she was so relieved that she had found herself sagging against the wall. She had made sure to wait for Michael and Jack so that they would reach there at the same time. She had gotten there at nine and had started working without taking a break because she wanted to leave before he came home. She did not want to see him; did not want to remember the feelings he had stirred up inside her.

It was already Thursday and the second week of November. She had planned on finishing his kitchen by Monday or Tuesday of next week but she did not know if that was at all possible. The place was huge, not as large as the main kitchen but still they had a lot to cover and both Michael and Jack not seeing the urgency, were doing it in a timely manner.

She had her life in order. She did not date because it meant putting some man in her son's life that maybe was not worthy of him and she had been too busy to even think about the physical side of a relationship. She had been doing well until last night when he had kissed her!

"Damn!" she muttered as the tile she had being putting up shifted slightly.

"You okay there, El?" Michael looked at her curiously.

"Yes," she said briefly, taking it off and positioning it better.

"Want to take a break?" Jack asked her.

"No, I am okay." She said dismissively. Just then Mitsui came in with Miki behind her bearing a tray with pastries and tea. It was a little after three and Elise was planning on leaving by five. "I am giving the order for you to stop working right now and let us take a seat and have some of these tasty treats left over from our book club meeting." She instructed the girl to put them on the countertop and gave Elise and her crew a pointed look.

"You don't have to ask me twice." Jack said gleefully, putting aside the tile he had just taken up and going to the sink to wash the dust off his hands.

Michael did the same and Elise realized that if she continued working she would look churlish.
"Okay, I guess it's time for a break." She said forcing a smile.

Mitsui ate with them and asked the questions about the work being done. She also told them about the book they had been discussing. She stood up and wandered around the kitchen, her sharp eyes taking in the pattern of the tiles. "You do excellent work," she told them, the remark encompassing all three of them. "I am glad you were recommended to me.

Although my son does not use the kitchen, he is going to love it."

"Will he be coming home shortly?" Elise asked casually.

"Oh no dear, he went away this morning for a few days. A sudden business trip."

Elise felt the relief coursing through her! Good, now at least she could really get the work done without wondering if he was coming home!

*****

She took her mother and her son out for pizza that evening to celebrate him getting all the words right that he had been asked to spell . The pizza place was jammed pack at that time of evening with parents and children having their meal.

She ordered a large pepperoni with extra cheese and mushrooms and Daniel dug into it eagerly. "Toni Ann got all her words right too, mommy," he told his mother as he took a huge bite of his pizza. "Do you think her mommy is taking her out for pizza?"

"Or maybe she is at home cooking her a nice meal," she teased him, ruffling his curls.

"That's boring," he said making a face. "Grandma, why aren't you eating?"

Leslie had been toying with her slice of pizza and to Daniel that was a mortal sin.

"I am not feeling too well darling. I think I might have acid reflux." Leslie told him gently.

"What's that?" he asked with a frown.

"Something I ate does not agree with my stomach." She explained.

"You want us to leave mom?" Elise asked her in concern.

"Of course not! And spoil Daniel's celebration meal? I will just ask them for a spot of tea to settle my stomach and I will be fine."

They left the pizza place and walked around the brightly lit mall, slowly looking in at the stores that were still opened. It was almost Thanksgiving and all the stores screamed the words: 'Sale!' on the doors. It reminded Elise that she had to get some new winter gear for her son; he had outgrown the ones he had. He skipped along between the two women happily, and at one point dragged them inside a toy store.

"Can I have that train mommy, please?" he begged pointing to a large red and blue train surrounded by several smaller ones. People were milling around with their children, some looking at the merchandise and some purchasing.

"Don't you have enough toys?" she asked him exasperatedly.

"No," he answered promptly dragging her over to the display. A sales person materialized immediately with a smile on her very young face.

"See something you like?" she asked the little boy, sensibly not addressing the adults.

"Yes that train!" he told her excitedly, glad to have someone on his side. "Does it cost a lot of money?" he asked frowning. "I don't want my mommy to spend all her money, then we don't have anything to eat." His four year old voice was very intense and the adults around him looked at him in amazement that he could be thinking of something like that.

"Not very," the girl told him solemnly.

Elise could not help it; she had to buy it for him. He took the package from the sales clerk hands and insisted on carrying it.

"Quite an amazing kid you got there," the young girl commented.

"I know," she said with a smile.

They went home after that and she gave him his bath and some chocolate milk and made sure he brushed his teeth. "Mommy can I play with my toy train instead of you reading me a book?" he turned his large dark eyes up to hers pleadingly.

"Okay, ten minutes buddy and then it's lights out." She told him.

"Thanks mommy," he said and took it out of its package sitting cross legged on the bed. When she checked on him minutes later he was fast asleep the train tucked in beside him. With a tender smile she took it away and kissed his cheek, pulling the comforter over him.

Chapter 5

He called her when he came back. She had decided to take the weekend off because Jack was going out of town and she could see that Michael needed some rest. It had gotten bitterly cold overnight and she decided that she was going to clean out and reorganize her son's room and get rid of the toys he was not using. She had also promised her mother to re polish the countertop in her bathroom. She was in the bathroom mixing the paint for the wood, when her phone rang. "Hello?"

"It's Peter," he said briefly. "I would like you to have dinner with me tonight."

She looked at the watch on her wrist and realized to her surprise that it was almost five o'clock. Her mother had taken Daniel with her to the supermarket to get some produce.

"No," she said without hesitation.

"Why not?" he demanded.

"Because I am free to say no and not give you a reason Peter," she told him calmly, proud of herself in spite of the racing of her heart.

"I want to see you Elise," he said impatiently.

"And I said no." She wanted him to stop asking before she weakened and agreed. "You will see me when I am there to finish working on the kitchen."

"If you don't come out with me I am coming over. I would love to meet your son." He told her in a determined voice.

"You wouldn't!" she exclaimed in alarm.

"Try me." He said his voice soft.

"I will be over there shortly," she said before hanging up the phone. She was furious! Who the hell did he think he was? She put the cover over the paint and washed her hands in the sink, her expression mutinous. She was going to put an end to this once and for all! She was going to let him know that just because he had an itch to scratch it does not necessarily mean that she was at his beck and call to do the scratching. And how dare he use her son to get his own way!

She called her mother to tell her that she would be going out for a little bit and to tell Daniel she would be home shortly.

*****

She got there in record time, not even bothering to change out of the faded denims and black sweater she had dragged on over her white T-shirt. She had pulled on a baseball cap on her messy curls. She did not want him to get the wrong impression into thinking that she was going to dress up for him! She jumped out of the truck and marched up to the front door, wondering vaguely if his mother was around. As she was about to press the buzzer, the door was pulled open and he was standing in the doorway. She had never seen him in casual clothes before and she was taken aback at the loose black sweat bottom and black T-shirt he was wearing, and his feet were bare.

"Come on in," he said pleasantly.

She stepped inside but only because she was freezing. "You have some nerve! Do you think because I do work for you that you own me?" she was so angry that she was shaking.

"I missed you," he told her softly, causing her to stare at him, aghast. "I thought going away from you would make me miss you more but it only intensified it."

"You need to stop!" she wanted to sound authoritative but her voice came out wobbly.

"I can't," he backed her up against the door and for one wild moment she thought about running! It was too late! He bent his head and captured her mouth with his in a kiss so potent that she thought she was drinking strong liquor! She sagged against him, her hands coming up to brace against his chest. He deepened the kiss, fisting his hands into her hair and knocking her cap off in the process. She was drowning in the kiss and she could feel the desire blossoming inside her body, and with a sigh she spread her hands over his chest and then around his neck.

He lifted her petite frame easily and carried her towards his suite, never breaking the kiss. He put her down on the bed and stood there staring down at her. Her curls framed her face wildly and her lips looked like they had been bitten by insects; they were swollen from his plundering of them.

He knelt over her and pulled off the sweater and then the T-shirt and ran his hands over her breasts. "Peter," She rose up on her elbows and looked at him, not sure this was a good idea.

"Don't ask me to back off Elise, I tried that and it did not work." He told her hoarsely, bending his head to take a nipple inside his mouth. Elise let out a startled moan as the desire raged inside her. She gripped the soft sheets on the bed, her body arching towards him as he pulled her nipple inside his mouth. Every thought of leaving left her mind and all she wanted to do was to be satisfied.

He broke off the kiss and pulled her pants down. She had never been a 'girlie girl' but she had the very best taste in underwear, leaning towards lace and silk, loving the way it felt against her skin. He pulled down the black lace and then he got undressed and joined her on the bed. He framed her face with his hands and looked at her deeply. "I can't stay away" he told her before bending his head and taking her lips with his in a kiss that had her reeling! He eased up and cupped her breasts in his hand as he slide on top of her, his erection nestling between her legs. "Peter!" she gasped.

He released her lips and kissed her chin softly going down until he was sucking on her nipples, his hand easing her thighs opened. His mouth met his fingers down there and his mouth tasted her mound as his fingers worked their way inside her. Elise cried out in shock! She had never experienced such unbelievable ecstasy in her life and she felt her body exploding into tiny pieces.

He did not want her to come yet. He wanted her to wait on him, so he moved his mouth from her and he entered her slowly. He waited on her to adjust to length and width of him before he started to move. He moved slowly at first and then she wrapped her legs around his waist, his thrust became more urgent. He gripped her face in his hands as she closed around him tightly. He had taken the fact that he was very good with women for granted, but now with her, he felt as if this was his first time! He wanted more, needed more and he did not want to stop. He took her lips with his own, drowning out the voice telling him that she was not his type; she was not the type he usually goes out with. He would deal with that later.

Elsie felt the stiffness of her nipples against his smooth muscled chest as she moved against him urgently. She had been with Daniel's father several times and it never felt like this, not even close. They came together in a tumultuous explosion that had her calling out his name. He captured her cries with his mouth as he moved urgently inside her, his hands gathering up her hips to bring her closer to him. He did something unusual. He moved out of her shortly after and rubbed the tip of his soaking wet penis over her mound, his eyes holding hers. She was still in the throes of her orgasm so her body had still not recovered yet, and to add this on top of it, she was shuddering uncontrollably.

He moved off the bed abruptly and pulled her off with him. The bed was on a dais with three steps leading down, and he stood on the second step and took her into his arms, his fingers going inside her wetness as he captured her lips with his. He wanted her to stay, but he knew she had to go home to her son. He knew that even so, she would not consider spending the night with him.

She came against his fingers, her mouth clinging to his. He removed his fingers when he was sure she was finished, but his mouth was still on hers. He wanted her again, and with a groan he lifted her and placed her on his erection, holding her steady as he thrust inside her desperately. She held on to him as she returned his thrusts, her arms around his neck. She came with him again and he had to hold her still as she bucked against him frantically! He held her against him, his body shuddering from the powerful orgasm that had rocked both of them. He walked with her back towards the bed, his penis still buried inside her. He did not want her to leave, God! He did not think he could stay in his bed if she was not in it, not after this.

"I have to go," she said huskily as he kissed her cheek gently. He was still moving inside her slowly.

"I want you to stay," he told her hoarsely, already feeling himself hardening inside her.

"I have my son to go home to Peter, and I do not stay away from him." She glanced at the clock at the bedside table and realized that it was already minutes to eight.

"Stay a little bit more," he urged her, one hand reaching between them to finger a nipple.

"You don't play fair," Elise moaned as she felt the desire coursing through her.

"I know," he told her bending his head to take her lips with his.

*****

It was almost nine o'clock when she left. He had told her that his mother had gone for the night to visit with a friend. He walked her out to the vehicle and she hastily strapped herself in and turned the key in the ignition, wondering what she was going to tell her mother and son about where she had been.

"When can I see you again?" he leaned against the window to stop her from driving away.

"I'll be here on Monday Peter," she said, impatient to leave.

"You know what I mean Elise," he countered. God he was handsome, she thought, her heart skidding as she took in his tousled hair and his piercing dark eyes. But handsome had gotten her pregnant and left her with a kid to take care of, so she knew better.

"You mean when we can have sex again?" she asked him coolly, deliberately hardening her heart.

"You know that was not what I meant!" his tone was impatient. "I want to take you out and I want to meet your son."

"Not going to happen," she told him coldly, releasing the brake. "We had sex and that's it."

"You really think that was all there was to it?" he asked her frowning, stepping back.

"As far as I am concerned, that's all it was Peter." She told him grimly and without waiting for him to respond, she gunned the engine and drove off leaving him staring after her.

She had lied to him and to herself. It was not all sex. It had been more than that but she was not stupid enough to fall for that again. She had learned her lesson the very hard way!

*****

They were waiting up for her when she got home, both of them engrossed in a cartoon movie. "Mommy, where were you?" her son demanded as soon as she entered the room and took off her coat. He was already in pj's and he looked clean and well scrubbed. Her mother was in her nightgown with a robe over it and she wondered if she had kept them up.

"I had to go see a client honey," she said with a smile, sitting down and pulling him on her lap. She hated lying to him and she cursed the fact that she had allowed Peter to break through her resistance. "You had your chocolate milk?"

"Grandma made it but not as good as you," he told her in a stage whisper.

She laughed and her mother shook her head. "That's the last time I make it for you, Danny boy," Leslie teased him.

"Grandma, you and mommy are always telling me to speak the truth, so I am doing that." He said with a straight face.

"Is that so?" Leslie descended on him with the intention of tickling him and he squealed with laughter and buried his face into his mother's bosom. Elise left them playing and went to take a shower. She could still smell him on her.

She stood under the shower and let the water beat down on her from her hair down. She leaned against the tiles and closed her eyes, her body shivering as she remembered what he had done to her and how he had felt inside her. Her nipples hardened and she whimpered, remembering how his mouth had felt on her body! She wanted more! She had told him it was just sex but to her horror she had considered spending the night with him! He had gotten under her skin and she could not allow that!

*****

"How did the giant build his house up in the sky mommy? The clouds are not hard enough to build a house is it?" he asked her curiously. She had read 'Jack and the Beanstalk' to him as she cuddled with him underneath the sheets. Her guilt at leaving him for so long to go and have sex with Peter had prompted her to spend a little extra time with him.

"Good question sweetie. But I supposed, as in your cartoons, even the impossible can happen and this is just make believe." She told him. "Now it's really bedtime now, so how about a kiss for your old lady?"

He grinned at the term 'old lady' and gripped her tightly around her neck. "I am so glad you are my mommy," he whispered against her cheek.

Elise felt the tears coming and she had to blink. "And I am so glad you are my son."

That night in bed she found herself staring up at the ceiling, her thoughts in turmoil. She certainly could not allow anything or anyone to get between her relationship with her son, no matter what her body was saying to her.

*****

She deliberately went to the house after nine on Monday so she did not have to see him. Mitsui greeted them at the door and invited them to come and have breakfast with her. "I hate eating alone and Peter left so early this morning, not that he usually stays for breakfast anyway." She complained as she led the way to the newly remodeled kitchen. "I have been eating breakfast in here ever since it has been fixed up," she said with a delighted smile. The sun was coming through the windows that had been added and gave the room a cheerful glow. It felt strange to be back here after Saturday night and Elise found herself looking towards his suite of rooms.

They were served scrambled eggs and bacon and toast and although Elise had eaten a hurried meal of bagel while her mother and son had chocolate chip pancakes, she ate everything on the plate including the fresh strawberries with cream.

They went immediately after breakfast to go into the kitchen they were finishing up and Elise felt his presence so potent in the rooms that it was as if he was there. She stared at the spot where he had first kissed her and her body tightened in desire. This has got to stop! With a determination borne out of desperation, she went straight to work and tuned out everything else, including the conversation between Jack and Michael. Mitsui had told them that she sat on several charities and they were trying to raise money to build a new wing for the hospital. Hamasaki Imports had already added a wing for the children with special needs but they wanted to add a wing for children with terminal illnesses where their parents could come and stay with them during the time they were in the hospital. "That's a good idea," Elise had told her, looking at the woman with new respect.

"I am not just a wealthy woman who does nothing else but shop, my dear," she had told her in amusement.
"I never thought that," Elise had protested.

"Didn't you?" Mitsui had teased, her eyebrows raised. She had come to like the down to earth girl who, in spite of her beauty, did not use it to advance her career and she liked that she never seemed impressed by their wealth.

"Maybe a little," Elise had told her with a grin.

They were almost finished the kitchen and to her surprise she realized that they could probably start on the next kitchen tomorrow.

*****

He came home just as they were packing up to leave at five thirty. She had hoped that they would have left before he came home but she had not realized that the time had gone so far.

Her breath caught in her throat as she saw him standing in the doorway. "Mr. Hamasaki sir," Jack said straightening respectfully. He greeted them cordially then turned to her. "May I speak with you a minute please?"

She thought about refusing but she could not very well do so, not with Michael and Jack watching. "Of course," she said stiffly, handing her tool belt to Jack. "I'll meet you guys in the truck."

He waited until they had left and came towards her. He was wearing his dark blue business suit, red shirt and a blue and red tie and he looked like what he was: a rich and successful man. "I wanted to call you yesterday." He told her softly stopping right in front of her.

"I am glad you didn't," she forced herself to stand her ground.

"I am not going to go away Elise," he warned, reaching up to tuck a stray curl behind her ear, his hand lingering on her cheek. There it was again, the betrayal of her body to his.

"I need to leave," she said hating the catch in her voice.

"And I need to be with you," he used both of his hands to cup her face. "What are we going to do about the situation?"

"That's not my problem." She was breathing too fast and he was too near, she thought in panic.

"Oh but it is," he muttered, bending his head to capture her lips. The hands she had reached up to grab on to his, tightened as she opened her mouth helplessly beneath his, her self control slipping. His mouth softened against hers and she sank into the kiss, meeting his tongue with hers. With a groan he pulled her closer to him bringing up her petite body to meet his. He explored her mouth hungrily and felt his penis hardened to rigidity as he molded her body against his. It was when he reached inside her shirt to cup her breast that she realized that she had her crew outside waiting for her and that if she allowed him to continue she was going to beg him to take her right there and then.

She tore her mouth away from his and backed away. "Don't!" She cried out as he made to pull her back into his arms. "I have to leave." She was breathless and shivering and she hated that he had such power over her body.

"Tell me when I can see you," he stood in front of her refusing to let her leave until she had given him something concrete.

"I don't know!" she cried out in frustration, she could not think with him standing right there.

"I can't accept that Elise," he told her firmly.

"What the hell do you want from me?" she asked him angrily.

"I want you," he told her bluntly. "And as much as you try to deny it, you want me too. So deal with it." With that he strode out of the kitchen leaving her staring after him angrily!

Chapter 6

She gave in and went out with him. She insisted on him taking her to little known restaurants because she did not want the publicity. Two times he flew her in his private jet to have dinner out of town and she found she had started lying to her mother and her son because she told them she was dealing with a client out of town so she would pack something to wear for dinner with him and changed in the vehicle. "Don't judge me" she had told him as she slipped into the little black dress and hurriedly put on some lipstick before they went inside the restaurant. "I am not ready for them to know yet."

It was in Mid December before they had an argument. They were at a restaurant having dinner when he asked her again. "I want to meet your son."

Elise looked up at him, her heart hammering. They had been together for more than a month now and she had been sneaking around the back of the estate to go to his suite almost every night to be with him. Whenever they were making love she forgot about everything, until after she would get dressed in a hurry and leave. He would walk her out and she knew he wanted her to stay, she wanted to stay as well but she had a child to think about.

"I am not ready for you to meet him yet." She told him firmly.

"When?" he demanded, putting down his fork and giving her his full attention. He looked so achingly handsome with his straight dark hair combed back from his forehead and the black cashmere sweater and the blue shirt he had on underneath.

"I don't know when!" she said her voice rising a little bit.

"I can't do this anymore Elise. I want to go public with our relationship and I am not one to hide what I am doing." He told her the finality in his voice striking into her heart.

"You have nothing to lose! You are rich and untouchable and I have a son who looks up to me for example. I refuse to let him get involved with a man I am screwing!" she knew she had said the wrong thing as she saw the expression on his face. "I didn't mean that."

"Yes you did," his voice was quiet and she felt dread fill her heart. She did not want to lose him because she was actually starting to feel something for him but her son came first. "I need to leave so I will take you home." He paid the bill and took her hand to help her up.

"So that's it?" she rounded on him furiously as soon as they were in the car. She always parked the truck at a spot where he could let her off and she get in her truck. He would always follow behind her until she got home and did not leave until she was inside. "Because I am not yet ready to introduce my son to you then it's over?"

"I am not used to sneaking around Elise and I-"he stopped short and then continued. "I am giving you some time to think about it."

They continued the rest of the way in silence with Elise fuming. How dared he barged into her life and now when she was starting to feel something for him, he was backing her into a corner! Men! She thought furiously, getting out of the car and going to her truck without a word to him. Inside she sat there, knowing he was not going to drive away without her moving off. Good, let him sit there! She thought with a pout. She hurriedly changed out of her clothes and pulled on her jeans and sweater and then with a shrug she drove away watching him through the mirror.

She was right wasn't she? She argued to herself. What kind of irresponsible mother would she be if she let the man she was sleeping with be involved in her son's life? But wasn't he more than that? A little voice argued inside her head. She could not answer because she already knew the answer to that question!

*****

Peter pulled inside the circular driveway and cut the ignition. He had wanted to get out of the vehicle and force her to see the truth. He was not just someone she was having sex with; he was more than that, much more. He had wanted to tell her that he had fallen in love with her but he had stopped himself just in time, she would have probably laughed in his face. He wanted her, child and all, and he hated that he had had to resort to be sneaking around like he was a damned teenager sneaking out of his parents' house.

He had to let her see reason somehow, even if it meant not seeing her for a little while. It was for the best. So why did he feel as if his heart was tearing out?

*****

Elise missed him! It was like a permanent ache inside her and she kept expecting him to call her. She found herself wishing that she had not finished the work at the house.

She called his mother one day. It was nearing Christmas and Daniel was home on holidays and driving them crazy asking about getting a tree and what was Santa bringing him for Christmas. The work had slowed down somewhat and she and the guys had redone a bathroom on Monday, and today being Thursday they had not gone out much.

"My dear good to hear from you!" Mitsui said in delight. She had kept in touch with her and she had told her that they had gotten the funding for the new wing of the hospital. "Why don't you come over with your family for Christmas Eve? We are having a big function here at the house. Peter is having people from his office over and several business associates and it would be good if you could make it." At the sound of his name her heart stuttered.

"I am not sure what I will be doing," Elise said hesitantly, knowing there was no way she would ever be there.

"Think about it and let me know my dear. I would love to see you and finally meet that delightful son of yours." Daniel had spoken to her over the phone and she had fallen in love with him.

"I will call you." She told her.

She stood there looking out the window at the starkness of the winter day, her eyes faraway. The bare trees reflected what she was feeling and she felt a shiver go through her as she remembered the last time they had made love. He had trailed his fingers down her flat stomach and down her pubic area, lingering on her mound as he watched her face.

"Tell me what you want?" he had asked her huskily, his fingers dipping inside her.

"You know what I want." She had gasped, her legs widening.

"I want to hear it." He had insisted and she had told him.

He had come on top of her and entered her forcefully and as she wrapped her legs around his waist he had thrust inside her urgently.

She closed her eyes and wrapped her arms around her body. She missed him so much!

"Mommy I want to go out to the park," Daniel bounded inside the room, interrupting her thoughts. She forced the smile on her lips as she turned towards him. It was almost three in the afternoon and her mother had gone to visit a sick friend in the hospital.
"It's freezing out honey; this is not the time to go to the park." He had been inside his room playing with his toys and she had been trying to make space for the Christmas tree they were planning to go and look at later. "And besides we are planning to go look for a Christmas tree later remember?"

"I still want to go to the park." He said stubbornly, his lower lip hanging down.

"How about I play something with you?" she suggested.

"Like what?" he asked her.

"Anything you want."

"Like hide and go seek?" he asked hopefully.

"Okay." She said after a slight hesitation. "You hide and I will count to ten and I will come and find you." He raced off immediately and she started counting. When she reached ten she called out: "Ready or not here I come."

She pretended to search for him underneath the bed in his room. She searched in the other rooms and even in the kitchen. "Where is Daniel? I cannot find him." she called out loudly, even though she saw his sneakered feet peeking out of the closet. He finally came out and said triumphantly. "Mommy I won! You did not find me!"

They continued playing until it was time for them to have supper and by that time Leslie had come home.

She helped her mother to clean up the kitchen and got her son ready to go to the tree lot.

*****

"How about this one?" Elise pointed to the tree closest to them. It was probably too big for their living room but what the heck!

"It's huge Mommy!" he exclaimed looking up at the large willow, it's branches spreading out. There were several people milling around and children dressed in warm clothes darting from one place to another. She kept a firm hand on Daniel, needing to know where he was at all times.

"So, we are going to have fun decorating it." She told him with a smile. She was just about to go and find a sales person when she heard his voice calling her name. "Hello Elise," he was right behind him and she could not believe it.

"That man knows your name Mommy," Daniel told her as she turned to face him.

"Yes honey, this Mr. Peter," she did not bother to tell her son his last name.

"Hi, it's nice to meet you Daniel." He took off his black leather glove and held his hand out for Daniel to take. The little boy looked up at his mother as if for permission and she nodded. He shook Peter's hand solemnly.

"How do know my name?" he asked curiously.

"Your mother told me all about you." Peter told him with a smile. His eyes drifted to her. She had stood there looking at him in his dark blue sweater and dark blue pants and black cashmere coat and she had wanted to launch herself into his arms. Thank God her son was here!

"How did you know I was here?" she asked him quietly.

"I stopped by the house and your mother told me." He said.

"Mommy, can we get our tree now?" Daniel tugged at her hand impatiently.

"You already picked out a tree?" Peter asked the little boy.

"Yes we did and it's huge! Mommy said it probably won't fit inside our house." Daniel said in excitement.

"Mind if I tag along?" he asked the little boy, not looking at Elise.

"Can he Mommy?" Daniel looked up at his mother and she nodded.

"Okay, come on," he dragged her along and Peter followed behind.

The sales person came along just then and they paid for the tree and to her surprise, she saw Peter instructed a man who worked in the lot to put the tree in the back of the truck.

She hesitated after she had strapped in her son around the back seat. "What are you doing here Peter?"

"I am surprised you ask." He said with a lifting of his brow. "I am not prepared to wait any longer Elise. I have told mother about us and I am not going anywhere. I'll follow behind." He told her briefly going towards his parked vehicle.

She fumed at his highhandedness but felt her heart thudding inside her chest. He was back and he was not going anywhere!

"Mommy, who is that man?" her son asked her curiously as she got in and started the vehicle.

"He is a friend sweetie, a very good friend." She adjusted the mirror and watched as he made the turn to follow behind her. With a smile on her face she headed on home.

*****

He came in with them and took the tree out of the truck, letting Daniel hold a limb which pleased him so much that he told Peter that he wanted him to stay and decorate the tree with them. "That's up to your mother," his eyes met hers from the other side of the tree. Leslie had just come into the room. "Ah, Peter you found them." She looked at her daughter curiously but did not say anything. "Danny, why don't you come with me into the basement and let's go dig up those decorations?"

"Yeah!" he said jumping up and heading out with his grandmother.

"Your mother is very understanding," Peter commented. He made no move towards her but she felt as if he was touching her. "So am I staying to help with the decoration? I am tall enough to put up the star."

"Have you ever decorated a tree before Peter?" she asked him.

"I can learn," he said softly, coming towards her. She tried to move but she could not, she felt as if she was glued to the floor.

He took off the furry hat she had worn to go to the lot and brushed back the untidy curls from her face. "I missed you so much that I could not function," he murmured, cupping her cheek.

"What are you doing?" she whispered trembling. "My son, my mother-"

"They will be taking their time to look for those decorations, unless you want to come home with me after we finish dressing the tree?" he parted her lips with his thumb.

"I can't," she whispered. With that he pulled her into his arms and took her lips with his hungrily, like a starving man finally finding food! She clung to him, the thought of her son and her mother in the basement disappearing from her mind. She had missed this, missed him and she leaned into him, her arms going around his neck as he brought her body closer to him.

"Come home with me," he said raggedly, pulling her away from him.

"I can't," she cried out in frustration.

"After Daniel is asleep, please, and I promise to bring you back before he wakes up." His hands were clenched at his sides. "Please, I need to be with you."

"Okay," she said her voice tremulous.

"I have to go." He said tightly.

"You said you would stay for the decorating," Elise reminded him.

"Please tell him I am sorry I had to go but I cannot stay like this," he came nearer to her and took her hand and placed it on his rigid penis. Elise closed her eyes and squeezed him gently, already on fire for him. "If you don't come Elise I am coming to get you." He warned her hoarsely and hauling her into his arms he kissed her brutally before letting her go.

She was still recovering when her mother and Daniel came back up ten minutes later. "Where is Mr. Peter?" he asked curiously, his little arms laden down with brightly colored bulbs and crepe paper.

"He had to leave honey; he said to tell you he was sorry." Elise said, not willing to meet her mother's curious look.

"Okay," he said with the resilience of a child.

They had fun decorating the tree and her mother left for a little bit to get them hot chocolate and cookies. It was a weary trio who went off to bed at minutes to ten. Daniel could barely keep his eyes open as she kissed him goodnight.

She went to take a shower and dressed carefully in a matching red lace bra and panties that looked great against her skin and pulled on denims and a light blue sweater before taking a deep breath and going into her mother's room. Leslie was sitting in front of her dressing table and braiding her shoulder length hair. "Going out?" she asked mildly, meeting her daughter's gaze in the mirror.

Elise sat on the bed heavily. "There is something I should have told you for some time." She paused as her mother turned around to face her.

"I am sort of seeing him."

"You mean Peter Hamasaki?" Leslie asked her.

"Yes." Elise sighed. "He had been telling me he wanted to meet Daniel and to let us go public but I told him no and he gave me an ultimatum."

"What are you afraid of?" her mother asked her gently, getting up and coming to sit beside her on the bed.

Elise looked at her in surprise; that was the last thing she expected her mother to say.

"What?"

"Honey, we both know you learned your lesson from that time five years ago. Not all men are like Daniel's father, and you should not let that experience stop you from experiencing the joy of true love." Leslie told her clasping her hands.

"Wait a minute mom," she protested. "I am not sure what it is yet, we are just going into this thing and we are taking it slow." She paused. "I am going over to his house and I just want you to know where I am when I am not here."

"Go right ahead, and honey, do not close yourself off from love. You'd be surprised at the joy it brings."

So she had gone to his house without fear of being found out.

He was waiting for her when she got there and without a word he lifted her into his arms and took her inside his bedroom.

*****

"Daniel, settle down honey," Elise told her son for the fifth time as he wandered around the large room examining everything. She had finally told Peter yes to their coming over and even though she had not wanted to take her son, he had insisted. He had closed his office building for the holidays and he had invited them over.

Mitsui had been delighted to see them and had taken charge of Daniel immediately giving him a tour of the place and showing him the kitchens his mother had remodeled. Peter had gone into his study to take a call and Elise had been left in the living room until both Mitsui and Daniel came back. His eyes shone with excitement as he examined the various 'treasures' as he put it, lying around.

"Oh leave him be my dear, it is so good to have a child in the house again." She looked at Elise curiously. "Hopefully there will be more in the very near future."

"What?" Elise looked at her startled.

"I have been hankering for grandchildren for ages and now I am a little closer to getting my wish, starting of course with Daniel." Mitsui said with a genial smile.

Elise felt her heart thudding inside her chest and making her excuse, she asked Mitsui to mind Daniel for her and she went to find Peter. He was just coming off the call and turned towards her. "I am sorry about that, I-"

She did not let him finish. "Did you tell your mother that I was going to have a child for you?" she demanded, her large dark brown eyes flashing.

"No I did not, that was mother being who she is," he said quietly, watching her as she shoved back her curls impatiently. "But would it be such a bad idea?"

"You want me to have your child?" she looked at him incredulously.

"I want more than that actually," he told her coming in front of her and holding her arms with his hands. "I want to spend my life with you and Daniel and whoever comes after."

"Are you nuts?" she asked him pulling away from him.

"I hope not," he told her ironically, his heart sinking. "Where did you think this was going Elise?"

"I don't know!" she said in frustration, turning away from him. "I like things the way they are right now. I am not ready for whatever it is you have in mind."

"You mean marriage?" he asked her softly coming up behind her. He turned her to face him and tilted her chin to look at her. "I want you in my life permanently and I don't like the idea that you live elsewhere. I want us together."

"I can't think when you are near." She whispered.

"I want you to say yes," he whispered bending his head and claiming her lips in a soul searching kiss!

Chapter 7

She went to the Christmas dinner at his house. She had told him she did not think it was a good idea but he had insisted on it. She had not given him an answer about what he had asked her the day before and she knew he was waiting on it.

He had bought Daniel a gift. It was an electric train set that she knew must have cost a lot of money but she had not said anything to him. He had also bought her diamond earrings and her mother he had given a lovely cashmere jacket which she told him she would treasure. Daniel was so delighted with his present that he refused to play with anything else and had pleaded to keep it in his room. He had told 'Mr. Peter', a polite thank you before racing off to play with his train set.

"I was contemplating whether or not to get you some tools, but I decided against it," he teased when she opened the box tentatively. He had seen her looking at the box and wondering whether or not it was a ring. He wanted to ask her what her answer was but he did not want to pressure her too much. He was afraid to lose her.

Now she was at the Christmas dinner with him. She had bought a dress for the occasion; a red wool with a deep plunging neckline and long sleeves. It was ankle length and the most expensive thing in her closet. She had on the diamond earrings, and her hair was caught up in a neat chignon at the nape of her neck. He had also bought her a white cashmere jacket and had put it around her when he came to pick her up. He had stared at her as soon as she opened the door, caught by her beauty. She had on a little bit of make-up that served to highlight her beauty.

He kept her close to him as he went around the room greeting business associates and friends and making no doubt about whom she was to him. He introduced her as a family friend but she knew he wanted to say so much more.

Mitsui came over at one point and took her away, "Stop monopolizing Elise, Peter. I am sure she is quite bored with all the business talk going on."

She had gone off with his mother and sat with her and her friends as they sipped champagne and discussed the different charities they were a part of.

It was after midnight before everyone left and she waited for him to take her home. His mother had told her goodnight and went on up to her suite.

"Stay," he told her as he closed the door behind a business associate he had been talking to.

"I have to go home," she told him.

"Please," he murmured. He had pulled her into his arms and she looped her arms around his neck. "Call your mother and tell her you will be home later today."

"Daniel-"she began. She wanted to be with him so badly.

"Daniel is going to be sleeping in late." He interrupted her. He had backed her against the door and his hand reached inside her dress. She was not wearing a bra because the dress had not allowed it. His fingers feathered over her already stiff nipple. "I need to be inside you." He murmured, ducking his head and capturing the nipple he had been touching. Elise cried out softly and sagged against the door as his mouth pulled at the nipple hungrily. He lifted her dress and found out she was not wearing panties. He groaned against her lips as he felt the smoothness of her skin. "I want to take you right here."

"I'll stay,'" she gasped against his mouth. Without a word he lifted her and took her to his suite.

*****

"What is this one called?" Daniel pointed to a dinosaur with a very long neck and a long tail. They were at the children's museum; for he had said that he was going to treat Daniel for the day. It was the second day of January and they had gotten snow the day before.

"It's called a Brontosaurus, and that one over there with three horns is called Triceratops and they were plant eaters." Peter told him. He held on to Peter's hand and he patiently let him drag him to the different displays.

Elise wandered a little way behind them and watched her son with the man who had started to mean so much to her. He was so patient with him and despite his busy schedule and the fact that he ran a billion dollar company that did not stop him from calling him and talking to him.

They ate hot dogs and hot chocolate in the restaurant inside the museum. It suddenly occurred to her that she wanted this and she was sure her son wanted it as well. He caught her looking at him and she had a feeling he knew what she was thinking.

He took them home at five and Daniel raced inside to tell his grandmother about his very exciting day. "Are you coming over?" he asked her, lifting a hand to put a wayward curl behind her ear.

"No," she shook her head. "Not tonight."

"How long are you going to do this for Elise," he asked her impatiently.

"You agreed to give me time," she reminded him.

"I am dying here," he told her huskily. "Whenever I have to leave you and go home to my place I feel as if I can't stand it."

"I just want you to be sure about Daniel as well as me before you commit yourself to something permanent. If it's just me that's fine but it's my son as well."

"And I would like him to be my son too." He told her softly.

Page 122

She stood there in the circle of his arms staring at him.

"Speechless?" he asked her wryly. "That's a first." He lifted her chin and kissed her lingeringly on the lips. "I will expect you tomorrow." He said before he left.

Daniel rushed back inside the room looking for him. "Where is Mr. Peter?" he asked looking around very disappointed.

"He had to leave honey, but he said to tell you he will see you soon." Elise told him with a smile. Her lips were still stinging from his kisses and she wanted so much to be with him. She was having a hard time concentrating on what her son was saying.

*****

"Mother you are home," Peter made the observation as he hung up his coat on the coat hanger in the living room.

"Why wouldn't I be?" she asked him mildly. "How was the outing?"

"It went well. Daniel was quite excited about the dinosaurs." He said with a smile. He joined her on the wraparound leather sofa and realized that she had been reading 'Gone with the

Wind'. "Book club assignment?" he asked her with a raised brow.

"I can read aside from the books recommended in the club you know," she told him huffily. "But yes, we have a meeting on Friday and we have a new member so we want to impress her."

He shook his head and got ready to leave. Mitsui laid a hand on his arm, not wanting him to leave just yet. Ever since he had become involved with that delightful girl Elise, he had been different, more approachable and she liked that. "When are you going to tell her?"

"Tell her what?" he asked, having an idea what she was talking about.

"Tell her that you are head over heels in love with her and her son?" she asked him mildly.

"You knew?" he sat back against the cushion.

"Darling I have eyes and I happen to know you," his mother said dryly.

"She is not ready for that yet," he said briefly, looking at the hands clasped loosely between his thighs. "She needs time."

"And you are getting impatient." It was a statement not a question.

"I am," Peter said with a rueful smile.

"She has been through quite a bit darling, remember that." Mitsui put aside the book she had been reading. "Have I ever told you the story of your father and me?"

"What story?" he looked at her curiously.

"The story of how we got married."

He shook his head. "Wasn't it an arranged marriage?"

"Yes," she said with a shake of her head. "Both our parents were from Japan and they came to America together so many years ago. His parents as you know had a son and my parents had me and we were the only children for both of them. It was agreed that we would get married when the time was right. I went to college and met and fell in love with a Caucasian boy and was hell bent on marrying him. Only I did not know that he was the college Lothario and that he was sleeping with all of my friends. I gave him my innocence and he dumped me the next week. I came home devastated and I could not tell my mother and father what had had happened or else I would have been disowned. Your father noticed how disconsolate I was and asked me what was wrong. I did not tell him at first but he kept asking and I finally did. He saw the shame and took my hands and told me that no matter what, he still had the utmost respect for me. He never touched me until our wedding night and he was very patient with me until I realized that I had fallen in love with him."

Peter stared at her in amazement. He had always assumed that both his parents had been married because they had been forced to do so. He had always seen his father as a taciturn man with few words but he never realized what they had shared.

"That's a beautiful story," he told her softly, reaching out to take one of her slender hands. "You are telling me to be patient with her because of what she has been through."

"Clever boy," she said with a grin, patting his hand. "She will come around, believe me."

*****

Later that night as he sat on the edge of his bed contemplating the story his mother had told him, he felt himself yearning for her even more. Her lingering scent of something strawberry was faint but present and he saw her every time he looked at his huge king sized bed. He loved her so much he could not breathe and he was frightened at how he felt about her. At first he had been prepared to tolerate her son because he was in love with her but he had fallen in love with the little boy and had no problem accepting him as his own. He needed them and if he had to wait then so be it, because he wanted no one else!

*****

"Honey I thought you were sleeping!" Leslie exclaimed as she came upon her daughter in the kitchen. "What are you doing up?"

"I could not sleep so I came out to have a cup of tea to see if that would help." Elise said wryly.

"Ah, affairs of the heart," Leslie said with a brief smile as she joined her, sitting on a stool beside her. "What is it you want honey?"

"What do you mean?"

"Do you want to spend the rest of your life living in the past or do you want to grab the future with that beautiful young man with both hands?"

"It's not that simple mom, there is Daniel to consider." Elise said staring down at the liquid in her cup.

"And Daniel loves him. What else are you worried about?" Leslie asked her.

"I don't know!" she said honestly.

*****

Peter took them to the movies the following Saturday. It was almost the end of January and the snow was piled up on the side of the road. Frozen was showing and he told them he was going to take them..

"Have you ever been to the movies?" she asked him as soon as he came to pick them up. He had been incredibly patient with her and had not asked her about marrying him or wanting her to come and live with him.

"When I was a child." He told her with a smile. He helped Daniel with his coat and the boy stood still and let him. Elise marveled at how well behaved he was when Peter was around.

He bought a huge bucket of popcorn and hot dogs for all of them. He had invited her mother as well but she had told him that she had plans of her own.

Daniel sat absorbed in the movie while Peter had his arm around her. She tried to resist at first, feeling strange because Daniel was right there but he had no intention of letting her go and then with a resigned shrug she rested her head on his shoulder.

This felt right and good, she thought. They were like a little family and Elise wondered why she did not give in and tell him yes. What was holding her back? She loved being with him and whenever she was away from him, she missed him like crazy! What was holding her back? She closed her eyes as she remembered how she had cried in his arms when he made love to her, how she had cried out his name as he thrust inside her over and over again.

What was she waiting for?

Daniel was sleeping in the car on their way home. "Tired?" he asked her as she rested her head back against the headrest.

"More like I have been turned into a popcorn zombie," she told him wryly. She turned to look at her son sleeping in his car seat, still clutching his 'Frozen' package of complimentary toys. "He had so much fun. He is going to be sleeping late."

"So you are coming home with me?" he asked her lightly, glancing at her briefly.

"Yes," she told him.

He looked at her in surprise and his hands tightened on the steering wheel. "Good," he nodded, careful to keep his expression neutral.

She hid a smile and reached over to cup him causing him to swerve the car. "Don't," he said hoarsely, directing the car back into the lane.
"I wanted to get a reaction." She told him softly, her hand on his thigh.

"You always will." He told her huskily.

He insisted on putting Daniel to bed and tucking him in. The little boy remained asleep the whole time, even when Elise kissed him tenderly on the nose.

"Mom, I will be back in the morning." Elise told her. She had clothes over at Peter's house so she just picked up some fresh underwear.

"Okay honey. I will be seeing you Peter." She told them with a smile.

*****

"My dad forced me into the business," she told him with a laugh. They had just finished making love and she was spread out on his chest with his arms around her. "When I was a little girl I always tagged along behind him and asked him a million questions about what he was doing. From that early age he started grooming me to take over."

"He probably saw your potential from that early age and decided to hone it." Peter murmured. He was making circular motions on the small of her back. "My dad had me reading the business section of the papers each morning while we had breakfast and would tell me what was happening in the

Page 131

company. He would let me come over to the office after school and when I was on holidays I worked there as a regular employee. It helped that I was fascinated by it."

She rested against his chest and felt the steady beating of his heart and closed her eyes in contentment, knowing that she felt at home with him.

"Tell me about Daniel's father," he asked her suddenly.

Elise stiffened and lifted her head to look at him. His piercing dark eyes met hers directly.

"Why?"

"I want to know what I am up against. Were you in love with him?" he asked her, his hand tensed against her body.

"I thought I was," she said after a little bit. "He was the first and only man for me besides you and I was swept off my feet. After he left and I realized that I had let down my parents and myself I was devastated." She looked away from him. "But I was determined to prove to them and myself that I would make it and I would be a good parent."

"Have you ever heard from him?"

"No," she shook her head. "Sometimes I feel bad for Daniel; because a child needs his father, but I am glad he has not come back."

"I want to be his father," Peter told her, his hand coming up to cup her cheek.

She stared at him for a long moment, her heart constricting at her words. "You are rich beyond what I can imagine and you are handsome. You can get any woman you want. I am a working girl with a son, why me?"

"I asked myself the same question when I first met you," he told her with a whimsical smile. "I guess the heart wants what the heart wants." He held her gaze with his.

"What are you saying?" she whispered.

"I am in love with you, and I have been in love with you since the first time I saw you sitting on the floor in the main kitchen." He told her.

"You don't know me, you don't know us!" she said agitatedly, moving out of his arms. She was still naked and he lay there propped up against the pillow staring at her exquisite beauty.

The kind of work she did had toned her body. and without being muscular it was finely honed and looked healthy and strong. "What if you discover later that you have made a mistake? A child is involved, so we cannot afford to be frivolous."

"I love you! Did you hear that part?" he sat up and reached for her reluctant body. "I am not going anywhere Elise, so if it's time you need for me to spend with you and Daniel then you have it. I am in charge of a huge company and I am usually busy but I promise that I will never be too busy for you both, trust me on that."

Elise sank against him, her body shivering against his. "I am scared," she whispered.

"I know," he murmured. "But I will never hurt you or Daniel, I promise you that."

*****

"You actually cook?" she asked in amusement as she saw him with an apron around his narrow waist. He was dressed in loose pants and a T-shirt and he was barefoot. He had invited them over for dinner and had decided to cook the meal himself. Ever since that night when he had told her that he was in love with her, he had been trying to prove to her that he was not going anywhere. He had had to go away on a business trip to Japan for three days and he had called her everyday and asked to speak to Daniel as well. She had started another project which was keeping her busy: One of Mitsui's friends had seen what they had done with the kitchens and had hired them to remodel her bathrooms and two kitchens as well.

"I cook," he told her. Daniel was in one of the bedrooms playing with some toys Peter had brought back for him.

"You are spoiling him," Elise had protested.

"I want to," he had told her briefly.

"I am doing sushi and hot dogs for Daniel, in case he does not like raw fish." He told her with a smile.

"I thought a rich guy like you would not even know how to turn on a stove." She said, propping her chin on her hand and watched him. He looked like he knew what he was doing and it fascinated her to think that he was actually cooking for them.

"My mother taught me to cook at an early age and even though I did not want to do it she told me it would prove useful in the long run." He grinned at her. "She was right."

Chapter 8

He took Daniel out to a baseball game. Elise had been working over and he called and asked her if he could do so. It was already February and snow had been falling for the past two days. "You said you want me to spend more time with him, remember?" he had asked her when she hesitated. So she had said yes, he was right and she wanted them to get to know each other better.

They had grown closer over the past two months. Daniel had asked if he could call him 'Uncle Peter' and he had looked at her. She had told him yes, feeling resentful and happy at the same time. Daniel had been only hers for years now, apart from the relationship he shared with her parents, and she was not certain if she was ready to accept him sharing the love with someone else.

They came home a little after eight with Daniel all excited and talking a mile a dozen about the time they had had and what Uncle Peter had bought him. He was wearing a baseball cap over his hair and said he was bursting with all the things he had to eat.

Elise saw them together and something triggered off inside her. She was the one who was supposed to make him bubble over with happiness like that! Not Peter!

"You look like you had fun." His grandmother teased him. He was still holding on to Peter's hand and usually he would rush into her arms, Elise thought, the jealousy rushing through her.

"Mom, could you take Daniel and get him ready for bed? I need to talk to Peter for a little bit." Leslie looked at her searchingly for a moment and then took her grandson's hand.

"Will I see you tomorrow Uncle Peter?" the little boy asked looking up at him.

"I am not so sure Daniel, I will let you know." He gave the boy a brief hug and then Daniel skipped away with his grandmother, talking excitedly about the game.

"Am I in trouble?" he asked lightly as soon as they were out of the room. "I did not realize it was so late and being a school night you must be upset. I assure you it won't happen again."

"He is my son, not yours!" she told him angrily, her eyes blazing. She was being unreasonable but she could not help the words coming out of her mouth. She felt cheated. He had not even hugged her when he was leaving with her mother.

"What?" Peter looked at her startled, his gaze narrowed. He was wearing a black sweater and black jeans and his cashmere jacket.

"You think you can come into our lives and just take him over? He has been my son before you and he will continue to be mine when you are gone!"

The silence that followed her outburst was awful! She wanted to take back the words but they had already left her mouth and she was not sure she wanted them to be unsaid anyway. Daniel had never not hugged her, he had never not run to her first and tonight he had acted as if she was not in the room.

"I have no intention of taking your son away from you and you would be a fool to think I am able to do that." His voice was quiet and Elise wished he was raging at her; it would have been better. "I love you and I happen to love your son, the fact that you cannot see past the hurt and pain of your past is something very regrettable. Please tell *your son*," he put the emphasis on the two words leaving her in no doubt that he wanted her to know that Daniel was hers. "Tell him that he can call me anytime, if you will allow it. Goodbye Elise." With a nod he left the room.

She stood where he had left her, looking at the closed door and realized that it also signified a close chapter in her life. He was not coming back and she was the one who had caused it.

"Aren't you going after him?" her mother's voice sounded behind her. "Don't worry your son is sleeping, thank goodness for that, we wouldn't have wanted him to hear what you said to the man that he is starting to think of as a father, would we?"

Elise felt the tears starting at her mother's cool and controlled voice. "He brought him back late," she said weakly, trying to justify her unforgivable behavior earlier.

"Really?" Leslie had come further inside the room. "And that was the only issue? That Peter took out that boy to show him a good time and brought him back a little over eight o'clock? I think the real issue is that you have deliberately gone ahead and destroyed a wonderful relationship that might have been. I have seen that young man take time out of his very busy schedule to prove to you over and over again how much the two of you mean to him and you have done nothing but fight it.

I have to ask myself why? Are you still in love with that low life that got you pregnant and left you to fend for yourself?"

"Of course not!" Elise said sharply, feeling the pain that her mother's words had invoked. "It's just that Daniel did not even come and hug me, it was all about Peter."

"I see," Leslie looked at her speculatively. "You are that insecure about your son's love that you don't want him to share it with anyone else?"

"No-"she started to say and then stopped. She sat down heavily in the sofa and stared straight ahead of her. "Ever since he was born I was the only parent and I thought I could love him enough for both parents. I never envisioned that I would meet someone who would want to be a part of our lives, because I was not looking for a relationship. I have never been in one and I don't know how to act now that I am in one. I keep expecting the other shoe to drop and I guess I was tired of waiting, so I did it myself."

Leslie took a seat beside her. She had seen how happy her daughter and grandson were since Peter had come into their lives and would hate to see her destroy something so precious. "You are going to have to fix it." She told her quietly.

"Because from what I heard from the conversation from his side, he is not going to make the first move."

"I can't, not right now." Elise said miserably.

"Then both of you will be losing out." Leslie stood up and without another word she left the room leaving Elise there, hunched in the sofa, the tears falling down her cheeks.

*****

Peter stared at the amber liquid in his glass with a dark frown. He had come in from his side of the house not wanting to have to answer any questions about the outing with Daniel from his mother. All the way back from her house he had felt the despair burning inside him. He had tried and he had done things he would never normally do because he had fallen in love and fallen deep. For the past several months, ever since he had met her, nothing else mattered as much as her and then he had met her son and realized that he needed them in his life, he needed them to be his family. At first it had all been about work and acquiring as much wealth as possible, until she had come into his life. He had tried to prove to her that he was not that creep who had gotten her pregnant and had left her to take care of their son; he was there for them, no matter what.

He swallowed the liquid down hastily and with a grimace of distaste he put down the glass on the counter. His eyes took in the excellent work she had done in the kitchen and knew it was going be a constant reminder of her. Everywhere in his suite was a constant reminder of them because she had some clothes in his closet, and there were toys strewn around the living room that Daniel played with whenever he was over here. He had refrained from getting in bed because it was a reminder of the way her body felt against his on that same bed. The many nights they had made love right there and how he had watched her sleep with her curls against her soft cheek. "You are watching me sleep," she had accused him one night waking up to see him looking at her.

"I can't help it," he had told her softly, bending to kiss her mouth gently.

He went into the living room and lay on the sofa, his eyes staring fixedly on the beautifully patterned ceiling. He was in for a very long night!

*****

"I want Uncle Peter!" Daniel said, his bottom lip trembling. It was a week since they had heard from him and she was running out of excuses as to why he was not coming around anymore. Mitsui had called her and asked why they were no longer coming around. She would ask her son, but he was not really around. Elise had not known what to tell her.

She was getting Daniel ready for school with the intention of going to finish the work that they had started at Michelle's place. "Where is he mommy? Why can't I see him?" he asked petulantly as she pulled the zipper up on his jacket.

"He is very busy now honey." She told him avoiding her mother's look. She had been having a hard time sleeping at nights and even when she was on the job she was finding it hard to concentrate and to make it worse she had to deal with the never ending questions from her son. She missed him so much that right now she felt like crying and she hated herself for the weakness she was feeling.

"When is he not going to be busy?" he son asked, stubbornly refusing to let it go.

"Honey, why don't you come with me in the kitchen and help me put some cookies in a bag to give to your teacher?" Leslie suggested to Daniel taking pity on her daughter. Elise sent her mother a grateful glance as her son ran towards her, and they went into the kitchen.

She took the opportunity to go into her bathroom and stared at herself in the large oval mirror. She had lost a little weight and there were bags underneath her eyes because sleep had eluded her since he had gone. She had hoped he would have called, even for Peter's sake, but he had not done so and she kept telling herself that it was for the best but that was a lie; both of them were miserable without him. Her bed felt strange and alien to her and she missed feeling his arms around her, she needed him so much that it had become a constant ache inside her.

She straightened up as she saw her mother in the doorway. "Has he calmed down enough for me to take him to school?" she asked wryly.

"You look like hell," Leslie told her bluntly. "You are pining over him and so is your son and if you are too damned stubborn to think about yourself, then think about that little boy in there who has finally found someone to call a father. I am taking him to school as I am going that way." Without waiting for her to answer she left, leaving Elise staring after them, dumbfounded. Her mother had never spoken to her that way before and she felt as if all her world was crumbling in on her.

But she was right! She was pining over him because she had gone ahead and fallen headlong in love with him! No amount of fighting was doing her any good and what was worse was that Daniel was involved as well. Fix it! Her mother had said but how as she supposed to do that? She had hurt him so much with her words that he was not even calling Daniel. How was she going to fix what was so broken?

With a sigh she sat down on the ceramic tile in the bathroom and put her head in her hands, the tears coming and not stopping! She cried as if her heart would break!

*****

"Get it done!" Peter said sharply, slamming down his hand on the table in the conference room. They were in a board meeting and the purchasing team had been a part of it as well. The cars they had gotten from Japan a week ago had been stuck at the wharf because of some mix up with the paper work and there were orders waiting to be filled but were not able to do so because of the hold up. Usually he would make a phone call to his source in that department and it would be sorted out, but since he had stopped seeing Elise he had no interest in anything, including the business. He wanted to hit someone, anyone.

"Yes Mr. Hamasaki sir," the hapless man in charge of the purchasing department said, and hurriedly left the room to see if he could somehow perform miracles and saved his job. "This meeting is over," he said crisply, not giving a damn if there were other matters to discuss. He just wanted to be by himself for a while.

The room cleared out except Martin Greendale, the Vice president of the company who remained in his seat. "What is it Martin?"

"I was about to ask you the same thing Peter," the well dressed middle aged man with dark brown hair streaked with silver said to him. "What is going on with you?"

"I don't know what you mean," Peter made as if to leave but Martin's voice stopped him.

"You are allowing your personal problems to interfere with the running of the company and that's not acceptable. We all have problems but we also have a company to run. You need to deal with the issue you have and get it together."

"It's my company," he reminded the man coldly.

"Correction, it's our company," Martin said standing up. "The others are afraid of you so much that they will not tell you the truth. I, on the other hand, do not give a damn; I have to tell you as it is. Deal with whatever you have to deal with and fast!"

*****

"Darling how very nice to see you!" Mitsui greeted her warmly. It was a little past three o'clock and she had asked her mother to pick up Daniel and had told Jack and Michael to continue without her. She could not concentrate anyway.

Mitsui ushered her inside the kitchen and poured them cups of herbal tea. Both helpers were somewhere else in the huge house doing some house work so they had some amount of privacy.`

"I messed up and now Peter is upset with me, and also Daniel and my mother." Elise said shakily, blinking back tears.

"I don't know what happened and I don't want to know, but this I do know. You have the power to fix it." Mitsui squeezed her hand gently. "I have barely catch glimpses of my son but the little I saw of him has revealed how miserable he is, and I have to tell you, he is very stubborn, so no matter how much he is suffering he is not going to call you."

"I know," Elise said with a glimmer of a smile. "Maybe he is not going to want to hear what I have to say."

"He loves you darling, and you are going to have to make him listen." Mitsui advised her. "You are going to have to find a way to do that."

"I told him some pretty hurtful things," Elise mused. "I was stupid and full of hurt and pain and anger and I said some pretty harsh things."

"Then make him understand that." Mitsui told her gently.

*****

She called her mother and told her to tell Daniel that she would see him in the morning.

"All the best honey," Leslie had told her.

She had had dinner with Mitsui and for the first time in a week she had eaten a full meal.

It was some minutes after six that she went up to his suite to wait for him. She had no idea what time he would be home but she was prepared to wait for the entire night if need be.

The place was immaculate as usual and she knew the helpers tidied up as soon as he left. She wished she had something to do to keep herself occupied and take her mind off things while she waited for him. So much for falling in love with a rich guy, she thought wryly; there was nothing left for her to do.

It was almost eight o'clock when she heard him in the hallway, her heart pounding inside her chest. What if he did not want to hear anything from her? She heard him put the keys on the side table and heard his footsteps as he made his way into the kitchen. She hesitated wondering if she should wait for him in the bedroom, but with determination she went after him. What she saw there made her want to cry! He was standing in the middle of the kitchen staring at the tiles and the expression on his face was tortured! "I will never hurt you that way again." She whispered. He spun around and saw her standing in the doorway. He quickly schooled his expression into one of indifference and waited for her to speak again. "I am sorry. I know it's not enough but it's a start and I need another chance for me and Daniel." He was still not saying anything and still not moving and for a moment she felt panic assailing her.

"I love you," she said quickly going over towards him. "I can't function and I don't want to live without you." She was standing right in front of him but still he just stood there. She reached out and touched his strong jaw. "Tell me it's not too late, please?" her voice was pleading and if she had to get down on her knees then she was prepared to do so. She started to do so when he finally reacted, gripping her arm and pulling her back up. "Don't!" he said harshly, his eyes sweeping her face.

"What are you saying?" he demanded, his grip almost bruising.

"I am in love with you, and Daniel and I want to marry you and come and live with you if you will have us." She told him tremulously.

With a groan he pulled her into his arms, his lips taking her with bruising force. Elise sagged against him, the relief making her weak as she returned his kiss with a passion that almost overpowered them! He swung her up into his arms and strode with her towards the bed putting her down on it gently. She had already showered and was in one of his T-shirts and she had no underwear on.

He stood there staring down at her as if trying to come to terms that she was really there and not a cruel figment of his imagination. He hastily undressed and climbed on the bed beside her pulling her beneath him and taking her mouth with his ferociously, one hand going between her legs to enter her. He was not gentle but Elise did not care, she needed the roughness as well. He thrust his fingers inside her rapidly, his mouth buried on hers. It was as if he wanted to punish her for making him suffer the last few days. He pulled out his fingers and reached for his erection. He released her lips and pulled the shirt over her head and then pulling her legs apart. He entered her gripping her hips and thrusting inside her with a force that almost had them falling off the bed. He gripped her hips and brought her closer to him; his dark eyes intent on hers. He had not spoken, but let his body do the talking as his thrust became more urgent. Elise clasped her legs around his waist, her eyes never leaving his face.

They came together, both crying out sharply as they shuddered together. He moved over her and took her lips with his, capturing her cries against his own!

Chapter 9

He got off her as soon as they had recovered and sat on the edge of the bed. Elise got up, her body still weak from what had happened between them and looked at him. There was no light in the room, just the light from the moon shining through the half opened drapes at the window of his bedroom. She crept across the bed and came up behind him, putting her hands around his neck. He closed his eyes and rested his head back against hers. "You have not answered me," she whispered in his ear.

He removed her hands and turned around to face her, his eyes scouring her face. "I never knew it was possible to feel such hurt and pain like I did in the last week," he smiled a little grimly. "I was determined to put you and Daniel from my mind even if I had to do it forcibly. I could not function at the office and I kept barking at the employees and the board members. I am afraid I have become even more unpopular than usual." He lifted his hand and cupped her cheek. "A member of the board advised me to get it under control and stop taking it out on everyone and I realized to my horror that the company I had worked so hard to build had been replaced and it was no longer as important as you and Daniel were. I can't go through that again Elise, because it almost destroyed me. It was then that I realized how powerful the hold is that you have over me."

"It's the same thing with me," she told him urgently, wanting to get through to him, her heart failing her as she listened to what he had to say. "I could not function at work and I kept making mistakes, simple ones that I never usually made. I almost sliced my hand off with a cutting tool and Jack had to take it from me. I am not myself without you and as much as it scares the living daylights out of me, I am prepared to accept this love I am feeling for you because I prefer to rather be scared with you, than to be miserable without you."

He rested his forehead against hers. "Oh Elise," he said brokenly. "I can't survive if you leave me, so please be certain."

"I am certain." She held him to her. "I am not sure about a lot of things but I want to be your wife."

With a cry he pushed her back on the bed and fastened his lips to hers in a hungry desperation that took her breath away! Reaching between them he put his semi erect penis inside her and she wrapped her legs around his waist. "I love you so much," she told him dragging her mouth from his to say it. "I love you!"

He pushed inside her and stayed still. "I am yours entirely," he told her hoarsely before he started moving inside her, holding her against him as if he would never let her go!

*****

They did not go to sleep until after one, and even so she slept on top of him with him holding her tight as if afraid she was going to leave during the night. He woke up back at six and made tender love to her that had her clinging to him and crying softly into his shoulder.

"Do you have to go in this morning?" she asked him huskily, raising her head to look at his beloved face.

"What do you have in mind?"

"I figured we could break the news to Daniel together. He has been pining for you too and he will be glad to know that 'Uncle Peter' will now be Daddy Peter." She told him huskily, pushing back his soft dark hair from his forehead.

He went still at her words and his eyes captured hers. "Are you sure?"

"I am sure," she told him with a smile. "There is a space on his birth certificate that's missing and waiting for your name. I want all of us to have the same last name, if you don't mind."

"If I don't mind-" he stopped as his throat clogged up. "I would be honored to share my name with both of you." He finished huskily.

"Good, let's go share the news with your mother," she told him, kissing him softly on the mouth.

*****

Mitsui squealed in delight and hugged them separately and then together. "Mother you are overreacting as usual," Peter said with a wry smile. He held Elise's hand in his and even when his mother was hugging them he had not let go. He had called his office and told them he would be late coming in and told his secretary to cancel his meetings for the morning.

"I am under reacting if anything," she retorted. She was still in her robe and was sitting around the breakfast nook Elise had set up, eating a boiled egg and some fruits. "Darling, we need to discuss the wedding."

"Of course, as soon as I go and tell my mother and Daniel about it." Elise told her with a smile.

"Don't worry, I will deal with everything and this place is large enough to keep a wedding. Now run along you two and don't keep that little angel in suspense." She said shooing them away with a happy smile.

"I hope you don't mind mother taking over," he looked at her in concern as they were on their way to her house. It was a little after seven and she had called her mother and told her that both she and Peter wanted to talk to Daniel so they would take him to school.

"So I take it everything is sorted out?" she asked, a please note in her voice.

"Yes," she had answered without going into details.

"Are you kidding?" Elise said with a laugh answering him now. "I hate doing that sort of thing so I am happy your mother wants to do it."

"Good," he said squeezing the hand trapped on his thigh. He had not dressed to go into the office but had put on dark blue pants and a red, ribbed sweater. She had put on denims and a forest green sweater she had left at his place and her hair was loose around her face. She had noticed him staring at her every few seconds and she guessed he liked her hair down.

Daniel raced to greet them the minute they opened the door and with a smile and a wave Leslie went back into the kitchen to give them some privacy. "Mommy, you were not in your bed when I came in this morning." He said accusingly.

"I know honey, and I am sorry about that but Uncle Peter and I had to sort something out." She told him gently. He was already dressed for school in his little red sweater and khaki pants.

"You stayed at Uncle Peter's house?" he looked at them frowningly.

"How about we tell you the good news your mom and I have to tell you?" Peter hoisted him up in his arms and sat on the sofa. Elise came and sat beside them.

"Tell me! Tell me!" he said impatiently bouncing on Peter's lap.

"How would you feel about my being your dad?" Peter asked him.

His dark eyes widened as he looked from one to the other. "You mean that you are going to get married to my mommy?" he asked his eyes rounded.

"Yes but we want to know if it's okay with you first." Elise said.

"I am going to be your son?" he turned to Peter.

"If you want to." Peter told him solemnly.

"I got my wish!" he cried flinging his arms around Peter's neck. He closed his eyes and wrapped his arms around the little boy's body, feeling so overwhelmed that he could hardly contain himself. "I wished that you would want to be my daddy but I did not want to ask mommy because she is always sad when I talk about that." He murmured, resting his head on Peter's shoulder. He lifted his head and looked at Peter. "May I call you daddy?" he swiveled around to look at his mother. "May I mommy?"

"Yes," she and Peter said at the same time.

"Yeah! Now I will not be the only person in my class not to have a daddy." He jumped out of Peter's arms to go and tell his grandmother.

She and Peter looked at each other in silent. "I never knew it affected him so much," she said with a catch to her throat. "Thanks for coming into our lives."

"The pleasure is all mine," he told her huskily pulling her into his arms.

*****

He could not sit still when they were taking him to school. He wanted to know what his name will be now and if he was still going to be Faulkner.

"You are going to be Hamasaki as soon as I get it sorted out," Peter told him indulgently, adjusting his mirror to look back at him.

"How soon?" he demanded.

"I promise that as soon as your mom and I get married it will be sorted out." Peter said patiently.

"When are you getting married?" was his next question.

"Let's see," Elise tapped a finger against her lip. "Now is February, we are thinking May." She looked at Peter to confirm.

"Or sooner," he told her softly.

"Where are we going to live?" he asked.

"At my house which will become our house. You want to come and pick out your room this weekend?" Peter asked him.

"Can I?" he squealed in excitement.

"May I," His mother corrected. "And yes you may."

They dropped him off and he insisted they come in with him so that he could show the rest of the kids and his teacher that he now had a mommy and a daddy.

*****

"You are very patient with him." Elise commented as they made their way from the school. The teacher had been very impressed when she saw who it was and had followed them to the car telling him that she was looking forward to him becoming a very active parent in the school.

"I love him, so it's easy." He told her lightly looking at her.

"I keep pinching myself often to find out if I am dreaming." She whispered.

"I know a better way to show you that you are not dreaming." He murmured huskily pulling the car off the road and coming to a stop. He took her into his arms and claimed her lips in a tender, heart stirring kiss.

*****

He picked out his bedroom. There were so many to choose from that at one point he was confused. There was an argument at one point because Peter said he wanted him to be close to them, and Mitsui was telling him that the rest of the house was bigger so he could get a whole suite by himself.

"I can have a bedroom and a bathroom and a play area for myself?" he asked his eyes huge. It was located near to Mitsui's suite of rooms and it had a delicate shade of powder blue. "I can have all of this?"

"You would be a little ways away from us Daniel," Peter told him.

"But we will be in the same house and my other grandma would be right here." He said to them. "Besides, when you are married you need to spend some time together." He added wisely.

"When did you become an adult?" His mother asked him teasingly.

"Don't be silly mommy, I am still a little boy," he said reproachfully before racing into his new rooms to look around.

"You don't have to use that bed. We can remove it and I can take you to the store and you can pick out any bed you want." Peter told him with a smile.

"Honestly?" he looked at Peter, his eyes round.

"Honestly." Peter echoed him in amusement. He launched himself at Peter and wrapped his arms around his waist. "You are the best father ever!" he told him.

The expression on Peter's face was priceless and Peter lifted him up and looked at him. "That's because you are the best son in the world."

Elise watched them, her eyes tearing up and then went over to hug them both!

*****

"Elise honey, what do you think about a morning wedding?" Mitsui asked as soon as she came downstairs. Peter had already left for the office and she had been spending most of her nights at his place. They had finished refurbishing Daniel's suite of rooms and he had picked out a bunk bed to replace the one there. His play room had shelves to stock his toys that Peter had insisted on buying him every chance he got. It was already April and the winter had officially ended with lots of rain and wind.

"I think that's good," she responded, wanting to get away. She had already gone for two fittings for her dress and Daniel's suit because he was going to be the ring bearer.

"What's a ring bearer?" he had asked them.

They had explained to him that it was a person who was in charge of the rings.

"Oh," he had said thoughtfully and nodded.

Peter had given her a diamond engagement ring which she wore around her neck reminding him that she worked in dust and all sorts of messy things so wearing a ring is not such a good idea.

"What about your wedding ring?" he had asked her.

"I promise that the whole world will know that I am married to you Peter Hamasaki," she had told him wrapping her arms around his neck. "I am going to be a very proud wife."

"What kind of flowers you want making up the bouquet?" Mitsui asked her as she shrugged into her spring jacket. She had a bathroom to remodel and both Michael and Jack were waiting for her outside. Peter had wanted her to use one of the many high end cars in the garage but she had told him she would use them when she was not working.

"I don't know," Elise said with a frown, looking at her future mother in law. It was Tuesday and she was meeting with her book club later today and they were all involved in the planning. She had been around the grounds of the sprawling estate and had blinked in surprise at the array of flowers planted in the gardens. The gardener was a middle aged African American man who had been with the family for years.

"Okay darling, I will figure it out," she said with a wave of her slender hand. The dress she had chosen was an off white one with old Venetian lace on the bodice and narrow at the ankles.

"Thanks Mitsui, you are an angel." She told her gratefully, hurrying out the door.

*****

"I can't believe you are marrying a billionaire," Jack commented as they drove out and headed towards the block where they would be working.

"Are we going to be losing our jobs?" Michael asked anxiously.

"What makes you say that?" Elise asked him negotiating a curve in the road.

"You won't need to work anymore." Jack commented. "You will be rolling in dough."

"I am still going to be working," Elise told them firmly "And you are not losing your jobs."

"I am sure Mr. Hamasaki will not appreciate his wife doing this type of work," Michael said not willing to let it go. "What billionaire would?"

She did not answer but went inside the house they were going to be working in. All throughout the day Elise thought about their comment and she realized that it was going to be business as usual for her and Daniel.

*****

"Are you going to expect me to quit my job when we get married?" she was sitting in front of the huge mirror in the room, rubbing cream on her skin. He was sitting on the bed watching her already in his pajama pants with his chest bare.

"Why do you ask?" he came and stood behind her, his eyes meeting hers in the mirror.

"Because the guys said something to me and I have been thinking about it as well," she murmured, bending back her head to look at him.

"It's up to you," his hands kneaded her shoulders and she relaxed back against him contentedly.

"I am aware that I am marrying a man with a public image and it just struck me that my lifestyle will have to be altered somewhat." She murmured.

"Do you mind?" he asked her curiously, turning her around to face him and crouching down in front of her. "I know it will be a big change for you and it will require that you do a lot of entertaining. Are you up for that?"

"I love you Peter, and whatever else comes with that I can accept that as long as I have you." She told him, reaching out to run her fingers through his dark hair. "I love my job, but I love you more and if it means I have to stop doing the rough work then so be it. I will make the arrangements and draw the designs if that's the case."

He pulled her down onto his lap and cradled her into his arms. "How did I get so lucky?" he whispered, resting his forehead against hers.

"I think that is my line," she whispered lifting his head and claiming his lips with hers. They were not able to speak for quite some time.

Chapter 10

Elise sat there staring at herself in the large oval mirror that was her dressing table. Even though she had protested that there was nothing in his suite that needed changing, he had insisted on adding furniture to suit her needs. He had spent the night in one of the other bedrooms at the west wing of the house and had crept out when everyone had retired for the night to come and be with her. After he had left she could not sleep and she realized wryly that she could not sleep without him. Her mother was also here at the house in her own bedroom and an adjoining bathroom. She had spent some time with her and Mitsui and the ladies from the book club who had insisted on throwing her a shower. Peter had been at work until late tying up some things there because he was planning on taking a week off to spend with her and Daniel.

"He is something else, that man you are getting married to," Her mother had told her as they sat in her bedroom after the shower and after Mitsui had retired for the night. "I hope you know that."

"I know that mom and sometimes it scares me how much I love him." Elise tucked her feet beneath her on the bed. It was almost nine o'clock and she had left Peter in his study going over some documents that needed his signature. "He's so wonderful to me and Daniel."

He had spent the morning touring the grounds with Daniel and showing him the pear shaped swimming pool, the tennis court and the basketball court. There was even a lane leading into the forest where a stream bubbled over stones and Daniel had exclaimed in delight as he saw a deer there drinking from it.

"I am so happy for you my dear and so sorry that your father is not here to see how well you turned out." Leslie said with a pleased smile.

"Thanks mom, I wish he was here as well." She had responded giving her mother a hug.

So now she sat in front of the mirror staring at herself, hardly daring to believe that in exactly an hour and a half she was going to be Mrs. Peter Hamasaki. The adoption papers were almost final and very soon her son would be their son and she felt the pleasure rushing through her at the thought. Mitsui had been true to her word and had done everything in terms of the arrangements for the wedding; from sending out the invitations to making sure the decorations, ice sculpture and a table was put out for the gifts. They were getting married on the grounds and the gazebo had been decorated with the colors they were using: lilac, peach and off white.

She had even gotten a hairdresser and a make-up artist to come in and take care of their needs in spite of Elsie's protest. "I can do my own make-up,"

"Really darling?" Mitsui had looked at her skeptically. "I have never seen you wear a stitch of make-up and not that you really need it being naturally beautiful, but we all need help every now and then, including you. And besides there will be photographers there to capture the moment in print and I am sure you want to look your best."

So now she was looking at the transformation in the mirror. Her hair had been clipped a little (because Peter had told her that he loved her hair the way it was) and had been swept on top of her head with a few tendrils lying against her cheeks. She had little rosebuds in strategic places in the front and sides and she was wearing drop diamond earrings and a matching necklace that Peter had given to her for her wedding present. The foundation that had been used on her face blended in with her coffee and cream complexion, and her dark brown eyes had been highlighted with skillfully applied mascara and eyeliner and she was wearing peach tinted lip gloss. She was only in her thin white camisole and transparent stockings and a garter belt around her thigh.

Mitsui and her mother came inside the room just then, already dressed. Her mother was in a lilac dress that looked very good on her and Mitsui had chosen to wear peach silk with her curtain of dark hair piled on top of her head and secured by chopsticks.

"Sweetie you look stunning!" Leslie said, stopping in the doorway and staring at her daughter, mesmerized.

"Stunning is not the word!" Mitsui clasped her hands together and looked at her. They had come to help her get dress as both of them would be accompanying her up the aisle. "You are absolutely sensational! Now let's get you dressed."

"Where is Daniel?" Elise asked.

"He is with Peter, remember?" her mother reminded her as she pulled the dress out of the plastic.

"I forgot," Elise stood up and stepped into the dress they held out for her. "Is it okay that I am nervous right now?" she asked them, turning around so that Mitsui could button up the many pearl buttons at the back.

"Of course it's okay darling," Mitsui told her. She had finished buttoning her up and she slipped into the matching shoes and turned to face them.

"My dear you are by far the most beautiful bride I have ever seen even inside a magazine." Mitsui breathed, staring at the girl in wonder.

"She is right, you are beautiful and I am sure that Peter will have eyes only for you. Not that he notices anyone else when you are around," Leslie said wryly, fixing the train behind her.

*****

The day had turned out beautifully; the sun shining brightly on the flowers in the garden; their scents vying for supremacy in the cool sunny April afternoon. Chairs had been put out on the lawn and all of them were already occupied. Peter was underneath the gazebo with Daniel at his side. Both of them were dressed in dark blue three piece suits with white roses in the lapels while Daniel held the velvet cushion containing the rings in his hands solemnly. The crowd stood to their feet as the wedding march started and they turned to look as the three women made their way up the aisle. The crowd let out collective gasps as they saw the bride and Peter felt his heart swelled inside him when he saw her. Her beauty wrapped around him like a silk coat and he felt the warmth from her reaching out to him even from that distance. The bond they shared was so strong that he felt himself being pulled towards her without even being aware of it. Without waiting for a signal he left where he was and met her halfway, giving her mother and his, brief smiles as he took her hand and placed it on his arm. He did not notice that Daniel had walked with him until he felt the little boy tugging on his pant leg.

He stopped and lifted him up in his arms and continued walking while the crowd cheered, putting him down when they reached the gazebo.

"Ladies and gentlemen, friends and families; we are gathered here this morning to witness the love between Peter Hamasaki and Elise Faulkner. The couple will be saying their own vows so I will step back and allow them to do so." The minister said smiling.

Peter took her hands in his and looked into her eyes. "Elise my love, my heart. I saw you the very first time and I knew I had found the one. The one who could make my heart race faster, the one who would come before all others, the one I want to spend the rest of my life with. I am weak and vulnerable where you are concerned and it scares me a lot, but as long as you are with me I am okay. You not only gave me you, but you gave me your son to be my son, and for that I love you so much that I can hardly breathe. I promise to love you, forsaking all others, cherish you and provide for you and our son in the best way I know how for the rest of my life, and if I die before you, you will never lack anything in life. I commit myself totally to you and you alone."

Elise gripped his hands in hers and could not find her voice. "You forced me to look beyond the hurt and pain of my past and looking past that, I saw you and what you represent in my life. I have found a love that I never thought it possible to make me feel this way. I cannot breathe when I think of you and when I am with you I am complete." She paused as he used a hand to remove the teardrop from her eye. "Daniel and I are so fortunate to find someone like you and I want you to know that I will obey you and respect you and honor you until the day I die. I love you Peter and I always will."

There was a hushed atmosphere in the audience and no one spoke for a little while until the minister clearing his throat asked: "If there is anyone here who thinks that this man should not marry this woman let them speak now or forever hold their peace." He waited a fraction and then turning back to them he said: "Peter Kenji Hamasaki, will you take Elise Fiona Faulkner to be your lawfully wedded wife?; to have and to hold through sickness and health till death do you part?"

"I do," Peter said clearly, his eyes never leaving hers.

"Elise Fiona Faulkner, will you take Peter Kenji Hamasaki to be your lawfully wedded husband?; to have and to hold in sickness and in health,forsaking all others, till death do you part?"

"We do!" Daniel's voice chimed out and everyone laughed in delight.

"Daniel has spoken for both of us." Elise said huskily, bending to give her son a hug. "I do,"

"The rings please, young man." The minister instructed. Daniel passed them to him and he took them and gave a set to Peter and the single band to Elise. "Please place the rings on her finger." Peter slid the rings on Elise's finger and Elise did the same for him.

"Now, by the power vested in me, I now pronounce you husband and wife. You may kiss your bride." He told Peter.

He pulled her into his arms and whispered against her mouth. "My wife," before he took her lips in a slow tender kiss that had her clinging to him as her body shivered against his.

"Can I call you daddy now?" Daniel asked tugging at Peter's pants. He broke off the kiss and bent to lift Daniel into his arms.

"I would have it no other way my son." He told the boy hugging him tightly.

"Ladies and gentlemen I now present Mr. and Mrs. Peter Hamasaki and their son Daniel," the crowd cheered and flashbulbs went off as they made their way down the aisle with Daniel between them.

*****

The reception was being held same place outside around the pool and chairs had been set up for that occasion. Elise had gone inside to change into a sapphire blue dress with flowing transparent sleeves, the fabric hugging her from her bosom down to her ankle. Mitsui had chosen the beautiful expensive gown for her to change into and she looked stunning in it. Her husband had come up with, her leaving Daniel in the care of both his grandparents.

"My wife," he murmured, coming up behind her as she reapplied her lip gloss.

"My husband," she said softly, leaning back against him with a sigh.

"I want to be alone with you so much that I can hardly stand it." He told her, cupping her generous breasts.

Elise groaned as his fingers touched her nipples and she felt the spark that flew through her body. He turned her around to face him and eased away the plunging neckline of the gown to stare at the flimsy camisole she had on. He pulled it away from her breast and bending his head he took the nipple inside his mouth.

"Peter," she gasped, holding on to him as his teeth grazed her nipple and caused her legs to weaken. He pulled it into his mouth and sucked on it hungrily, holding her steadily. "I can't" she muttered, feeling the orgasm coming on.

"I need you," he said hoarsely. "And I cannot wait." He went and locked the door of the bedroom and unzipping his pants he pulled her gown and slip aside, and entered her. He groaned as she closed around him and with a sharp cry he thrust inside her hurriedly from behind. Elise moaned and moved against him, matching his thrusts and it was not long before they came together, furiously both of them calling out each other's names as the orgasm crashed over them violently!

He cleaned her up tenderly as soon as they were able to move and then they went downstairs to where the reception was just about to start.

The toasts were made and then it was time for them to cut the cake. They fed each other and Peter took the tiny piece of cake from her mouth, his tongue touching hers and fanning the fire between them.
Then it was time for them to have their first dance as husband and wife and they danced to the Luther Vandross' 'Always and Forever' and he led her across the cobbled path gently, his

arms possessively around her small waist. Elise rested her head on his shoulder and closed her eyes. People were sitting around, eating, drinking and laughing but it was just the two of them, there was no one else as far as they were concerned. The song ended and they still stood there holding each other, unaware that they were being watched by almost everyone as they held each other close.

It was only when Daniel came over and touched her, tugging on her gown that they discovered that the music had ended. "The song is finished," he told them, looking up at them.

"So it has," Peter said in amusement, picking him up and going towards the table with Elise beside them.

*****

It was almost an hour later before they were able to leave. They had to spend some time reassuring Daniel that they would take him with them whenever they would go anywhere from then on.

"But why can't I come with you?" he asked tremulously as he sat on their bed while they were getting ready to leave.

"Remember I told you that when a man and a woman get married, they need to be by themselves for a little bit?" Peter asked him crouching down in front of him.

Daniel nodded, looking first at him then at his mother.

"Then, this is just the time I was talking about. Your mother and I need to spend some time alone together, but we promise that next time and every time after this we will never leave you when we are going anywhere." Peter promised him.

"Okay," he said with a lightning change of mood, jumping into Peter's arms. "I can stay with Grandma Leslie and Grandma Mitsui and they said they were going to take me to the park."

"There you go," Elise said, coming over to ruffle his curls.

"Okay mommy and daddy, have fun," he told them before racing off to find his grandmas.

"I can never get used to him saying that," he told her huskily as he stood up and took her into his arms.

"Get used to it." She murmured, putting her arms around his neck.

*****

They took the private company jet to Aubignan Bleu in France, a quaint and nostalgic country farmhouse settled squarely in the midst of vines, olives, and cypress and fruit trees. He had rented out the five bedroom villa for three days and they got there when it was just getting dark. The fresh country air was very evident and Elise stood there breathing in the non toxic air.

"How about a swim in the pool?" her husband suggested coming up behind her. Their bags had been put inside the biggest of the five bedrooms.

"Did we bring any swimsuit?" she asked him, looking up at him. She had never been to France before and she found herself looking at the lush countryside in fascination.

"We don't need any, we are entirely secluded." He said suggestively. "Are you up for some skinny dipping?"

"I am," she told him spinning out of his arms and started undressing. "Last one in the pool serves the other breakfast for the three days." She shimmied out of her panties and twirled it on her finger before flinging it in his direction before darting away. He caught her just as she was about to jump into the shimmering blue water and they jumped in together. "Tease," he said huskily pulling her inside his arms as they threaded water. "There is nowhere else like Paris in the Spring." He murmured. "Especially with the person you love."

"I agree," she looped her arms around his neck and he took her lips with his. He plunged his tongue inside her mouth and deepened the kiss, one hand going between her thighs to part the lips of her vagina and enter her. The combination of the water lapping inside her and his fingers set off an unbelievable sensation inside her and she shuddered against him, riding his fingers aggressively.

"Slow down baby," he whispered against her mouth.

"I can't", she gasped, catching his bottom lip between her teeth.

He groaned as the slight tinge of pain shot through him! He lifted her up against him and captured a nipple inside his mouth, pulling at it and grazing it with his teeth. Elise gripped his shoulders for balance, as well as to control the shiver invading her body. He released her and then placed her on his rigid penis and as she wrapped her legs around his waist he backed her up against the edge of the pool and started thrusting inside her slowly at first, his eyes holding hers, and when she started to move against him impatiently he moved deeper inside her, gripping her hips as his thrust became more powerful. He bent his head and took her nipple, sucking on it hungrily while he moved inside her with a desperation matched only by hers. The silence of the area was only interrupted by their muted cries as their bodies came together to make sweet music. He switched to her other nipple and they both felt the water swirled around them as the orgasm ripped through their bodies. They clung to each other and went under still holding each other, fused together by their mutual passion and the fire going through them!

They went inside only when they felt the pangs of hunger and went into the kitchen to forage for grapes and cheese and a bottle of Cabernet Sauvignon, where they drank most of the bottle that had been chilled for them. They were still naked and he made her lie down on the bed and dribbled drops of the liquid all over her body, where he proceeded to lick off every drop, causing the fire to start all over again! She was a trembling mess by the time he came over her and entered her slowly, stroking inside her, teasing her by pulling out and rubbing the tip of his penis against her mound. They spent the night making love until they fell into an exhausted sleep in the wee hours of the morning!

*****

They explored the countryside going into the town of Orange where they explored the ruins of an ancient Roman theater built in the first century. They made love under the sunlight after they had packed a picnic lunch where they drank wine and ate different types of cheese.

He took her to the enchanting bookstore: 'Shakespeare and Company' which was a book lovers' delight, where they listened to different poets recite what they had written.

They also went to La Cabanette where they munched on pizza with crusts so thin you could see through it and which had lots of toppings. He bought her Hermes and expensive chocolates and even though she protested at the cost, he reminded her that he had money and he wanted to spend it on her. She picked up Pralines, ganaches and fruit chocolates and a bag of coffee beans for her mother.

Their last night at the villa they spent in their bedroom, not bothering to put clothes on but after eating feather light croissants spread with Nutella and strong black coffee with orange juice.

"I promise we will come back very soon," he told her as the spread out on the bed after a dip in the pool. He had dried her hair and wrapped her in a thick white robe where they had eaten strawberries with whipped cream. "With Daniel of course." He added with a smile.

"He would love that," she said leaning back against him. "Tell me about your company." She said realizing that apart from what she had glimpsed in the paper about Hamasaki's Import and Export, she really did not know much about what her husband did.

"Our main focus is on high end vehicles but we mostly do business in Japan because that's where my dad started." He told her, his hand making circular movements on her back. "We started branching out in other things when I took over, like computers and anything to do with technology. My dad wanted to stick to one thing but I realized where the market was and decided to expand. At first the company was my 'baby.' I used to spend every waking moment trying to come up with new and innovative ideas to take us on into the future and I based my success on the amount of money I had in the bank, in stocks and bonds. I enjoyed it as well with expensive clothes, wines, going to the best restaurants, but I always knew that something was missing. I never knew what it was until I met you and then Daniel. You changed my way of thinking and my focus and I was no longer interested in making the next buck or trying to be one of the richest man in the country; You changed that and I can't tell you how much that means to me." She had lifted her head to look at him and his piercing dark eyes met hers. "You changed my life Elise and for that I would do anything for you, including giving up my life because my life means nothing without you in it."

Elise stared at him, her heart hammering inside her breast. She never thought it possible to experience something like this, something so rare and so special that she found herself wondering every time if it was real. "You changed mine too," she said huskily clearing her throat. "I was contented with normal and ordinary before I met you and my expectations were low. You showed me that I can dream beyond anything I could possibly imagine and that I deserve this type of love, the love you showed me that I never expected. You showed me extraordinary and special and for that I will always be grateful to you. I love you so much Peter that I don't know where you end and I begin."

"Then we are even," he told her hoarsely, reaching up to claim her lips with his in a kiss that left no doubt as to where he stood!

Chapter 11

"You commissioned Michael and Jack to build a tree house and a swing for Daniel?" Elise asked her husband in amusement. It had been two weeks since their trip to Paris and he had gone back to the office and she had gone back to work, scaling down a little bit on the manual labor. They had been getting an influx of jobs and she guessed with her name now being Hamasaki. She had had to hire two other persons and now operated from an office she had refurbished at the large estate she now called home.

"You do realize that I could very well do it without you having to pay them far more than the job is worth, don't you?" he was getting dressed for work and she had just came from Daniel's room where she saw to it that he was getting ready for school. The two girls there helped but Elise had become accustomed to taking care of her son that she still wanted to do it. Peter had also assigned a driver to take him to and from school.

"I thought you didn't do that sort of thing anymore?" he asked her his eyebrows raised. She came around to help him adjust his tie.

"I don't, well not really, but I would have done it for our son."
She said it naturally these days and was aware that it pleased
him immensely.

"And I know how busy you have been since we got back and
Daniel has been asking for a tree house since the weather is
so nice." He tilted her chin to look at her. He had noticed that
she looked tired and a little droopy and he was concerned.
"Are you feeling okay?"

"Why do you ask?" she held his hand and tried to sound
casual. The fact is, she was not feeling too hot and even
though she no longer did the rough work, the jobs had been
coming in fast and furious and she was having a hard time
keeping up.

"Because ever since we got back you have not been yourself,"
he told her bluntly. "I think we should call Dr. Carmichael." He
suggested.

She pulled out of his arms and went inside the bathroom. "I
am fine Peter, stop fussing." She said a little irritably.

"It's my job, I am your husband and you are the love of my life.
I am entitled to fuss," he had followed her inside the bathroom.

She had some designs to do and two jobs to look at but it was a little after eight and she felt as if she just wanted to go back to bed.

"I know honey, I am sorry," she said with a sigh. "It's just that I have been trying to catch up with the jobs we have been doing and I guess I have overextended myself."

"Give it up or cut back drastically, I don't care which, but you do not have to be doing all of this Elise," he told her tightly, his brow furrowed.

"You want me to quit and stay home? Doing what exactly?" she rounded on him furiously, feeling lightheaded and dizzy.

He saw her swayed and rushed over to grab hold of her. "I am calling the doctor," he told her grimly, feeling a little fearful.

"Will you stop trying to control my life?" she beat at his chest ineffectively but the effort was too much for her and she sagged into his arms.

"It's my job," he led her back to the bedroom feeling alarmed at how weak she was. "Are you pregnant?" he asked her, not daring to believe that she might be carrying his child.

"What?" she stared at him startled for a moment. They had discussed starting a family together but had said they would wait and give Daniel a chance to be with both of them before doing that. "No!" she said shaking her head. "I guess I am just tired that's all."

"You said it like it is not something you are hoping to happen." He said coolly. He had been trying to get her to stop working so hard, but she was not listening to him.

"Peter, can you not start with that?" she asked him wearily. "You know how I feel about you, about us, and I don't think I have to keep proving myself over and over again."

He sat beside her on the bed. She was an independent woman, that much he respected, but she was also his wife and he thought she would have given up the job entirely and gone into doing charity work but that was not her style and he had to respect her for that.

She came up on the bed and went behind him to wrap her arms around him, resting her head against his. "I will slow down." She told him. "I am going to take the day today and rest and I will start delegating from now on. How does that sound?"

He spun her around and put her on his lap. "That sounds better." He told her seriously. "I don't want to curtail your activities baby but I don't see the need of both of us working so hard, and besides, we have Daniel to think about."

"You are right," she rested her head on his shoulder. "I will stay home today and rest."
"Want me to stay with you?" he asked her, calculating in his mind what he had to do today. It was Monday and he usually met with the board and the sales team first thing in the morning.

She shook her head. "You can check up on me throughout the day. I promise I will stay home and won't even lift a straw."

"I'll take your word for it." He told her softly, bracing her back against the bed. Her curls had escaped the usual ponytail and was all around her beautiful face. He brushed them back tenderly. "I can't afford to lose you, I would rather lose anything else." He told her seriously.

"You won't lose me," she told him wrapping her arms around his neck and bringing his face down to hers. "I promise." She whispered as she took his lips with hers.

*****

"I come bearing lunch," Mitsui came inside the room with a tray laden with all sorts of delicacies. She had drifted off to sleep as soon as Peter had left but not before calling her crew to let them know that she was not available today. He had told his mother when he went downstairs that she was not to be disturbed and that something filling was to be brought up to her as soon as she was rested.

"Oh Mitsui you did not have to bring lunch up," she protested getting ready to swing her legs off the bed to take the tray from her mother in law.

"Oh no, please stay right where you are," the woman instructed firmly. "Your husband left specific instructions that you are not to lift a finger and I am following his orders."

"He's being melodramatic," Elise said with a sigh as she placed the table tray across her. There was a chicken sandwich, tuna casserole, slices of cakes, and lemonade.

"I think he is just concerned about his wife, darling." She sat on the bed and looked at her daughter in law. She looked much better now that she had gotten some rest and she no longer had the bags underneath her eyes. "You are married to a very powerful and wealthy man my dear, and as much as you want to pretend that your life is still the same, it is not." She paused as the girl ate and looked at her. "I was born in a middle income family and I had to readjust my way of thinking when I married Peter's father. He did a lot of entertaining of clients and I had to pay hostess, but the difference with me was that I thrived on playing hostess. I have a feeling you are different. Peter loves you and he probably won't tell you that you have to play hostess to his entertaining, but as his wife, I am sure you want to be supportive of him, am I right?"

Elise nodded. She realized that her mother in law was right and her mother had said the same thing to her just over the weekend. Her lifestyle will have to change because she was running in a different league now. He had told her that he had given her an expense account and her name was on all his accounts as well. He had also said that if she wanted anything all she had to do was to charge it to the account and she could buy anything she wanted for her and Daniel. She still had not done so and her side of the massive walk-in closet was still pathetically bare. Mitsui was right: He loved her too much to tell her what to do but it was her responsibility to start being his wife outside of the bedroom.

"I am going to find out when his next function will be," Elise said decisively.

"You don't have to darling," Mitsui told her. "Copies of his activities are sent to his home computer in his study so all you have to do is log on and find out."

"Then I need to do something else." Mitsui looked at her enquiringly. "I need to shop for an entire new wardrobe and do something with my hair."

"That's my department," her mother in law said with a wide smile. "I already know your measurements so leave it entirely up to me. You won't even have to leave the house."

*****

Elise watched in amazement as racks after racks of designer outfits were shown to her. She allowed her mother in law to choose and even tried on one or two of the numerous gowns. She did not look at the price tags and to her surprise she realized that there were none. They had thought of everything: including shoes and underwear and even coats for the various seasons. Mitsui had even ordered tons of clothes and shoes for Daniel. "So that he will not feel left out," she had said with a smile.

Next was her hair. The hairdresser who had done her hair for the wedding came by with his assistant, a thin anemic looking girl with purple hair. When they were finished and she looked in the mirror she was amazed at the transformation. She looked like a fashion model and not someone who should be remodeling someone's kitchen or bathroom.

By the time they had all finished; Daniel had arrived home.

He bounded inside; his eyes lighting up in excitement as he saw his mother in her bedroom. "Mommy you are home!" he said racing into her arms. "Hi Grandma Mitsui." He went over and hopped into her arms. The girls had finished packing the clothes in the closet and had gone to put away Daniel's clothes in his room.

"So how was school honey?" she asked him as he jumped from one place to another.

"It was okay," he said with a little shrug. "Gabriella had an accident and threw up all over herself," he said with a grimace of distaste.

"Oh the poor thing," Mitsui said in concern. "What happened to her?"

"She ate something bad, I heard the teacher said." He reported.

"Speaking of eating," Mitsui said standing up and holding out her hand. "How about we get you something to eat?"

"I am starving!" he admitted taking her hand. "Oh mommy, you look very pretty," he said as an afterthought before leaving the room. Mitsui flashed her a smile before letting him drag her away.

*****

Peter looked at the figures in approval and nodded to Michael Brady who was the CFO for the company. "We have made quite a bit of profit for the first quarter," he said looking at the sharply dressed thirty-three year old man seated in front of him. "You are very good at what you do and that's why I hired you. Now, I want you to tell me why is it your wife is calling my personal number and crying to me to ask you to leave the 'floozy' inside the office because she is seven months pregnant and cannot manage the stress."

Michael sat there staring at him dumbfounded. Marion had threatened to call his boss if he did not stop seeing her but he had not paid her hysterical threats any mind and he had still continued seeing Paula. The girl worked in the accounts department and had set her caps on him since the first time she had started working here six months ago, and as much as he had tried to end it, he could not resist her and now he had discovered he did not want to. His wife had found out about them because she had called the house asking for him. It had been a deliberate act on her part and he had spoken to her about it, but he had seen the smile on her face.

"She had no right," he muttered, staring down at his well manicured hands.

"She had every right." Peter leaned forward on his desk. "She is your wife man and furthermore she is carrying your child. Do you know what you are doing?"

"I can't resist her," he said plaintively, his dark blue eyes pleading with Peter to understand. "She came on to me and I could not resist, and now I am in so deep that I don't know what to do."

"If you do not deal with it I am going to have to let one of you go and I really do not want to lose you." Peter paused. "I am married as you know, and I cannot look at another woman. I don't see anyone else and I am positive it's going to be that way for as long as we live. You have to decide if this girl is more to you than your family, and you have to decide that pretty fast because I need it cleared up by now, and the end of the week. End it Michael." He said briefly.

"Yes Peter," he said humbly, getting to his feet. "What did you tell her?" he asked as he reached the door.

"I told her that she was not to worry, she was your wife and you were not foolish enough to throw away what you two have for a roll in the hay." Peter looked at him coolly. "I hope I am right."

He leaned back against the soft leather of his high back chair and looked at the closed door. He felt sorry for Michael, but he felt even sorrier for the woman at home, miserable because she has discovered that her husband had rejected her for another woman in her state of pregnancy. What would cause a man to cheat on his wife? He wondered. He knew that Maureen was an attractive woman but maybe pregnancy had changed her appearance somewhat. Elise would be the most cherished and loved woman in the world if he ever found out she was pregnant!

He reached for the phone and dialed her number, longing to hear her voice. "I am surprised you took so long to call back," her amused voice sounded in his ear. Even her voice turned him on, he thought closing his eyes.

"I was giving you half an hour space," he teased her "How are you?"

"I am fine Peter, stop fussing." She told him mildly.

"That's like telling me not to breathe." He told her lightly. "Still trying on clothes?" she had told him what she had done with his mother's help.
"I don't try on clothes Peter, you know that and you are going to have a heart attack when you see the amount of clothes bought. I am finally spending our money."

"Good to know and I am not going to have a heart attack, knowing you. I guess you are the one hyperventilating over the lack of price tags." He said shrewdly.

"You know me too well." She said dryly.

"I would never cheat on you." He told her suddenly.

"I would hope not. I would have no hesitation in cutting off what is supposed to belong to me alone." She told him.

"Ouch!" he said a smile in his voice. "No need for violence, I am all yours. Where is our son?"

"He is in the play room trying to decide which one of the many toys you bought him, to play with."

"Kiss him and tell him I will be home shortly."

"I will darling," she told him softly. "I was thinking: How about I cook for us later when Daniel has gone to bed?"

"Sounds like a plan." He murmured before disconnecting the call.

*****

"And the teacher had to take her to the bathroom and wash her off," Daniel said solemnly. He was sitting in Peter's lap and relaying the story he had told both she and his grandmother, but in greater detail.

"What do you think happened to her?" Peter asked him seriously. Elise loved watching them together. He treated Daniel like a person, always listening to him and making sure he thought about it before answering him. He was also very patient with him.

"I think she got sick because she ate something bad." Daniel told him. "I am glad I did not get sick and throw up all over my clothes, I would have felt so stupid."

"She could not help being sick Daniel," Peter told him.

"I know, that's what I told Benjamin. He said it's because she is a girl. But that's not true is it daddy?" he looked up into Peter's face, his eyes trusting and he felt his heart constricting as he looked down at the boy calling him Dad. He swore to himself that he would never do anything to ever hurt him and he would never let him down.

"No," he said softly. "It's not true."

He prepared Daniel for bed and told him a story and stayed with him while he drifted off to sleep. He stood there looking down at him in wonder. How could any father possibly not want their kid? He wondered.

*****

"How about tucking me into bed after?" Elise asked him as soon as he came into the sitting area. She had prepared spaghetti and meat balls and the table was already set with a bottle of Cabernet chilling in the bucket in the center of the table. His eyes widened as he took in what she was wearing. She had showered and changed into a sheer black teddy with the legs cut so high that he could see glimpses of her pubic area and the cheeks of her bottom. She had put on one of the brand new shoes with impossibly high heels that gave attention to her beautiful legs. Her hair was caught up into two pigtails and made her look like a mischievous teenager. "Ready to eat?" she asked him innocently as he just stood there staring at her.

"What are you doing?" he asked her hoarsely, finally finding his voice.

"I don't know what you mean," she pulled out his chair. "I am serving my husband of course." She indicated for him to sit. He did so, almost stumbling over his feet. She served him, making sure to bend over so that he caught glimpses of her breasts pushed up by the material. Next she poured the wine and gave it to him, and to make him even crazier she bent over to pick up the napkin that had fallen to the floor, causing him to groan as if in pain as he saw the lips of her vagina with the material caught in the middle.

"You are going to give me a heart attack." He said hoarsely, his body tightening with need.

"I would never do that," she told him mildly taking her seat at the other end of the table. "Bon appetit," she said, lifting her glass. She deliberately made some spill in her bosom. "Oh dear, I am such a klutz" she said, looking at him under her lashes.

With a groan he pushed back his chair and taking the glass from her, he hauled her up against him. "You tease!" he buried his head in her bosom and licked off the wine there before pushing down the material and latching onto her nipples. He lifted her and strode with her into the bedroom, his body tightening with every move. "Time to pay!" he growled as he laid her on the bed.

"Gladly," she murmured huskily reaching up to pull him on top of her.

Chapter 12

It was final! The papers had come through and Daniel was now Hamasaki. The summer had arrived with intense heat and bright promises. Elise had scaled down a whole lot and was involved in some of the charity work her mother in law was doing.

She stared at the birth certificate with the name added. Her son now has a name and a father who loved him like he was his real son. She remembered crying herself to sleep at nights when she had discovered that she was pregnant and with no father and no prospects and had spent days wishing and hoping he would change his mind and come back and had thought her life was over.

She was still in the bedroom and in bed while Peter was taking a shower; it was Saturday and they were going out to celebrate later today. He had brought the documents home last night and had given it to her and she had cried in his arms before taking it to show Daniel.

"So it means I am really your son?" he had looked at Peter after staring at the embossed document.

"You were my son before, but this just means that you are legally mine." Peter told him sitting on the bed next to him. He was well scrubbed and in his pajamas and had been watching cartoons. Peter had also bought him a flat screen television that he had installed in his play area with the promise that he would not get up in the night and turn it on.

"What if I cannot spell, Ha-ma-saki?" he asked, making sure to break up the name into syllables as he was taught to do.

"We will teach you." Elise told him.

"Can we celebrate?" he asked in excitement.

"We sure can," Peter had told him giving him a hug.

*****

Peter watched them both. He had absolutely refused to go on the merry-go-round but had opted to sit on one of the benches and wave at them each time they passed. Elise was sitting behind Daniel and smiled and waved each time she saw him. Her legs looked tanned and toned in lavender shorts and a lavender and white top that showed her skin. Her hair was piled on top of her head to combat the heat and she was wearing a pair of large gold hoops. She looked like a carefree hippie, just a little bit older than her son. He loved watching her and how happy she looked ever since they had been together. She had no make-up on and even though the make-up artist had left her tons of the stuff, she only wore them when she was going to some function or another with him. She had adjusted to the lifestyle easily enough and had taken having to laugh and make conversation with people she did not know into stride and he was so proud of her. Most of all she had scaled back drastically from doing the manual work, and although still very involved with her company, was prepared to step back and let her crew do the heavy lifting.

He had a family and he was so happy that he could not believe that he was the same person almost a year ago who had buried himself into work. Usually on a Saturday he would have gone to the office to put in a full day's work, but he was determined to make time for his family.

The ride had stopped and they came over. "Daddy, aren't you going to have even one ride?" Daniel asked him curiously.

"I prefer my horses to be alive Daniel," he told him gently, ruffling his curls. "How about something to eat?"

"That sounds great! I am starving." Daniel said jumping up from the seat.

"What else is new?" Elise said wryly, getting up as Peter reached for her hand.

They had hot dogs from a street side vendor and they strolled along the park and watched the ducks in the pond.

"I had often seen families going out and having fun together and wondered what it felt like," Elise murmured resting her head on her husband's shoulder and watched while Daniel stared at the ducks with their young ones. "I now know what it feels like."
"I never thought about it because having a family was the farthest thing from my mind before I met you," Peter said with a whimsical smile, his arms tightening around her waist. "I like the feeling."

"Have I told you lately how much I love you?" she asked him looking up at him.

"Not since we made love this morning," he told her huskily.

"I love you Peter Hamasaki," she murmured.

"I love you more," he whispered, kissing her softly.

*****

"They go well together don't they?" Leslie watched as her grandson and his adoptive father climbed into the large tree house that had been made with fancy windows and was large enough to sleep in. He had begged to have a camp night with a friend of his one day last week and both Peter and Elise had finally succumbed going out all hours of the night to check up on them. Peter had had an alarm installed on the house because he said it was better for his peace of mind. He did not want to know that while they were asleep indoors something might happen to him and even though the grounds were secured, he was still taking no chances.

"Yes they do." Elise agreed watching as her husband closed the door behind them. They were lying by the poolside and Mitsui had gone in to instruct the women on what to prepare for lunch as they had dedicated the day to just pure relaxation with family members. It was Daniel who had suggested it, and said that the Fourth of July instead of having a barbecue and inviting a lot of people, if it could just be family members alone.

"So how is Earl?" she asked her mother teasingly. Her mother had finally decided to start seeing someone and she had met him while doing volunteer work at the community center downtown. He was a retired firefighter and volunteered at the center as well and they hid it off a month and a half ago. Elise had met him when she had gone over to her mother's to pick up some papers she had left there. Leslie had told her that she was not ready for him to meet the rest of the family yet.

"He is okay," her mother said her eyes downcast and Elise was amused to realize that her mother was quite taken with him. He had seemed like a nice enough sort and she knew that both she and Daniel leaving at the same time had had an effect on her. "He is spending time with his children and grandchildren at their home for the day."

"You could have invited him over mom," Elise chided her. She felt the midday sun passing through the umbrella covering the chair and mildly remembering that she had forgotten to put sunscreen on.

"I am not ready yet," Leslie told her firmly.

"Okay, no rush," Elise closed her eyes and relaxed, determined to enjoy the day.

*****

Elise rode Peter's back in the pool while Daniel splashed water on them repeatedly in between playing with his rubber ducks. Leslie looked at the small family and felt, not for the first time, the glimmer of envy going through her. She was ashamed of herself because she had had a good marriage before her husband died and now the relationship with Earl has been going well. She had lied to her daughter, saying that Earl was spending time with his family. His family was all the way in Florida and he had hinted that he had wanted to come with her to meet her family but she had refused, telling him that she was not ready for that yet; he needed to give her more time. He had been hurt and she had seen it but she was not sure she wanted to put a permanent stamp on it just yet.

"You look like you are far away," Mitsui commented as she stretched out on the chaise lounge her daughter in law had been occupying. "They look so right together, don't they?"

"Yes they do." Leslie said quietly.

"Both of us lost the men we loved and it's not easy to bounce back from that no matter what people tell us." Mitsui's eyes met hers squarely. "I have not met a man who could add up to my late husband and to tell the truth I have not been seeking but I keep myself busy and I love being by myself and going about getting things done. I know you have questions about this man you have been seeing Leslie but it's worth it to see where it goes."

"My daughter and her big mouth," Leslie said wryly with a shake of her head.

"She wants you to have someone to talk to and be with when she is not around and I think she feels guilty because she now has a family and you are alone at the house." Mitsui told her.

"You are right," Leslie sighed. "I miss them and I especially miss my grandson running up and down in the house and asking me all sorts of questions. It's not easy being alone."

"You are not." Mitsui reached over to take the woman's hand. "You always have a place here and you have Earl, so if you are alone, you are the one who is doing it."

She squeezed Mitsui's hand gratefully and relaxed back against the chair with a smile. Two hours later she packed away some of the food and told them that she was leaving and her daughter hugged her tightly. "I am glad you are going to him, we all need someone." She whispered.

*****

"So we have the bounce about scheduled, and the clown as well; and the same person said that they can also provide a trampoline. Now what are we missing?" Mitsui tapped the pencil against her coral colored lips. It was July 15th and it was a birthday party for Daniel's fifth birthday and Elise had wanted to do just a small party with a few of his class mates and their parents but both Peter and Mitsui had insisted that it be a big event.

"What about the zoo animals?" Elise asked her dryly. They were in her office and she was doing up a design for a bathroom they had gotten earlier this week. Even though she had scaled down somewhat, she still did the design and left the manual stuff to Michael and Jack and the two others she had hired.

"Ah!" Mitsui said rising gracefully from the sofa. "The ponies for the rides for the children. Instead of getting a merry-go-round we should have real ponies' darling. Thank you." She said before hurrying out.

Elise stared after her in frustration. She had taken over completely and as usual had gone overboard with the planning. Her phone rang just then and she picked it up. "Your mother is doing it again," she told her husband as she answered the phone.

"You mean about the ponies?" Peter asked in amusement. He gestured for his secretary to close the door on her way out.

"You know about that?" Elise asked him in exasperation. "Baby, you are no better than she is. I wanted a small party but of course not, because we Hamasaki's' don't do anything small."

He felt the pleasure shoot through him at the way she included all of them together. "Of course we don't," he told her softly. "I miss you." He added softly. "I miss pulling on your nipples with my teeth and going inside you so deep that I touch your soul. I miss kissing you down there and sticking my tongue inside you."

Elise was silent as she tried to catch her breath. She felt herself going weak as his words stirred something deep inside her. "What are you doing?' she asked him huskily, feeling the wetness inside her panties.

"Having a conversation with my wife," he told her casually although his erection was practically boring a hole though his pants.

"You are going to pay big, mister," she threatened.

"Looking forward to it." He told her softly.

She looked at the clock on her desk and discovered it was almost two o'clock. She had time and besides, her mother in law had hired caterers for the event and Daniel was spending the day before the party with Grandma Leslie because the party was supposed to be a surprise.

She took a shower and sprayed on some of the expensive perfume he had bought her in Paris. She went into the vast closet and chose a short floral dress with thin spaghetti straps and flared waist that ended mid thigh and she teamed it with a pair of high heeled, strappy red sandals. She added sparkling diamond knobs and a silver chain with a diamond pendant that he had given her a week ago. She pile combed her hair into a neat chignon and looped it at the side of her neck and put some make up on.

Mitsui's eyes widened as she came outside where she was instructing some men to put some tables.

"I am going to take my husband out for a late lunch," she told the woman blithely.

"Of course," Mitsui said with a knowing smile. "Take as much time as you like, everything is under control here."

"Thanks," Elise said with a nod going towards the huge garage to choose a car.

"And darling, he is not going to be able to work for the rest of the day." Mitsui said slyly.

"That's the idea." Elise told her.

She drove the red corvette and felt the powerful engine turn over as soon as she turned the key inside the ignition.

*****

She took the private elevator up and said hi to the receptionist before going towards the secretary's office.

"Mrs. Hamasaki!" the woman stood up hastily staring at the stunningly beautiful woman in front of her. "He is on a call just now; shall I tell him you are here?"

"No, that's okay, I'll just go in. Thanks." She left the woman staring after her and went towards her husband's office. He looked up as soon as the door opened and stopped in mid-sentence. "I'll call you back." He told the person and replaced the phone staring at her wordlessly. She looked cool, elegant and so beautiful that he was speechless and he realized that he had difficulty breathing and moving.

She closed and locked the door and without a word, pulled the zipper on the side and stepped out of her dress. He watched, mesmerized, as he realized she was only wearing red silk panties that were cut low on her pubic area, and was still in the red heels.

"Please hold my calls." He told the secretary briefly and watched as she came around to sit on the edge of his desk her legs wide open.

"I told you I would make you pay." She told him huskily, placing one foot clad in the heels on his thigh.

"You sure did," he said hoarsely placing his hands on her thighs. "How can I pay?"

"Use your imagination," she suggested huskily.

He did. With a groan he put his head between her legs and sucked on her through the sheer material. Elise moaned and fell back on her elbows on the desk, her body tingling. He used his fingers to move away the material and thrust his tongue inside her urgently, gripping her hips to hold her while he used his mouth and his tongue to drive her crazy. He was very thorough as he licked her mound slowly and then thrust his tongue back inside her over and over again until she thought she was going to die.

He stopped but only so that he could remove her underwear and release his aching penis. He pulled her to the very edge of the desk and entered her forcefully, his eyes never leaving hers as she wrapped her legs around his waist. "You are the most unpredictable woman I have ever met." He told her hoarsely.

"Good, then you will never know what I am going to do next." She said softly moving against him urgently.

He took a nipple inside his mouth and bit down gently, causing her to cry out sharply, her body bucking against his. He took her on top of his desk, his penis thrusting inside her, stroking her and then pulling out only to stroke some more as the insides of her vagina pulled him. He increased the thrust and was glad that his office was sound proof as his grunt and her cries echoed around the room although he did not care who heard them. He would have taken her in the hallway!

He switched position, pulling out of her hastily and turning her around and entering her from behind. She cried out as he entered her from that position, his thrust hurried and impatient, and his fingers rubbing her stiff nipples. Elise could not control the reaction of her body! She felt as if she was imploding! Her hands clenched into fists on the desk and she felt the sobs rising inside her throat and she felt as if she could not get enough.

"I love you!" she cried out brokenly.

"I love you too," he leaned over her and sank his teeth into her shoulder and bit down gently. She exploded against him and she cried out. He came with her and pulled her back against him and fell on the chair, holding her as he spilled his seed inside her, his body convulsing!

She leaned back against him and turned her head to take his lips with hers in a slow tender kiss with his penis still buried deep inside her.

It was half an hour before they could recover enough to separate and even so he took her lips while they were in the bathroom freshening up. "You just ruined the rest of my work day." He told her, feathering light kisses on her cheek.

"Good," she murmured huskily putting her hands around his neck. They had finally gotten dressed and he had decided to leave with her because it was some minutes to four and the party was starting at five.

"I never saw this dress before," he had rested his forehead on hers.

"It was buried deep inside that vast room you call a closet." She murmured.

"I love it on you." He murmured huskily.

*****

Daniel screeched in surprise when his grandma Leslie took him over, dressed and ready. There were balloons of different colors and a big banner saying: 'Happy Fifth Birthday, Daniel' and tables loaded with food, and a separate one with a huge cake with his favorite cartoon character on it. His eyes widened as he saw the children from his class and the trampoline, the bounce-about and especially the ponies being led around by the horse groomers who had been hired for that occasion.

"Happy birthday sweetie," his mother said lifting him into her arms and giving him a big kiss. She had reached home and had changed into dark blue slacks and a red sleeveless blouse. Her husband had put on denims and a T-shirt.

"Mommy, I am a big boy now," he protested wriggling out of her arms and looking to see if his friends had been watching.

"Never too big for your parents, I hope," Peter said to him in amusement, ruffling his curls.

"No," he hugged Peter's legs before racing off to join his friends.

"How quickly they grow up," Mitsui said with a dramatic sigh as she came over to join them. The pool was available for whoever wanted to take advantage of it and the clown was making both parents and children laugh with his antics. Some had gone on to the ponies and some of them were bouncing on the trampoline. The caterers were moving around and serving the parents. Just then Leslie came over with Earl and introduced him to Peter and Mitsui. "Nice to finally meet you," Peter said to the tall strapping man with black wiry hair graying at the sides and a kind smile on his chocolate brown face. "Make yourself at home." He added.

"Thank you." Earl said with a smile and he and Leslie went off to mingle with the rest of the guests.

Peter and Elise went and greeted the parents and he held her firmly at his side as he greeted their guests.

Later on as they sat on one of the chairs. He looked at his son on the pony clutching the reins, his laughter ringing out and he felt the happiness bursting inside him.

"Thank you." He said softly holding his wife from behind.

"You are welcome," she told him, holding his hands against her waist and leaning back against him. She was home.

The end.

If you enjoyed this ebook and want me to keep writing more, please leave a review of it on the store where you bought it. By doing so you'll allow me more time to write these books for you as they'll get more exposure. So thank you. :)

Get Free Romance eBooks!

Hi there. As a special thank you for buying this book, for a limited time I want to send you some great ebooks completely **free of charge** directly to your email! You can get it by going to this page:

www.saucyromancebooks.com/physical

You can see a the cover of these books on the next page:

These ebooks are so exclusive you can't even buy them. When you download them I'll also send you updates when new books like this are available.

Again, that link is:

www.saucyromancebooks.com/physical

Now, if you enjoyed the book you just read, please leave a positive review of it where you bought it (e.g. Amazon). It'll help get it out there a lot more and mean I can continue writing these books for you. So thank you. :)

More Books By Mary Peart

If you enjoyed that, you'll love Another Man's Child by Mary Peart (sample and description of what it's about below - search 'Another Man's Child by Mary Peart' on Amazon to get it now).

Description:

Sophia's having a hard time.

Recently pregnant by her cheating (now ex) boyfriend, fired and living back with her mother, she doesn't feel like she has a lot going for her.

But when she gets hired as a temp by one of dashing billionaire Christopher Tang's companies, things look like they might be turning around.

Christopher falls for Sophia almost immediately, and her being pregnant by another man doesn't do anything to deter him. However, with Sophia's ex still causing trouble, and her doubt about her relationship with Christopher increasing as fast as her belly, will their new relationship hold up?

Want to read more? Then search 'Another Man's Child Mary Peart' on Amazon to get it now.

Also available: Their Convenient Baby Plan by Katie Dowe (search 'Their Convenient Baby Plan Katie Dowe' on Amazon to get it now).

Description:

High-powered PR rep Jessica has everything she could want in life.

Well, almost.

What Jessica would love is a child, but with her career taking up so much of her time she doesn't know how to have one.

Enter Joel; a handsome billionaire whom Jessica meets as a potential client, and a man who might just have the solution to her problem.

Joel also wants a child, and when he finds himself immediately attracted to Jessica's classic beauty and blunt personality, he thinks she might be just the right person to be the mother of his child...

No strings attached!

But will their arrangement stay purely business?

Or will it turn out to be more than both Jessica and Joel had ever bargained for?

Want to read more? Then search 'Their Convenient Baby Plan Katie Dowe' on Amazon to get it now.

You can also see other related books by myself and other top romance authors at:

www.saucyromancebooks.com/romancebooks

CPSIA information can be obtained
at www.ICGtesting.com
Printed in the USA
LVOW01s2017210716

497259LV00015B/180/P